Praise for *Mansfield Ranch* by Jenni James:

"Another endearing Austen adaptation! Every volume in the series has been a joy to read, and *Mansfield Ranch* is no exception." – Pinhead1, Amazon Reviewer

"Can't get enough! I absolutely love Jenni James!!! And all her Jane Austen remakes. But especially *Mansfield Ranch.* It had me snagged from the beginning to the end and I re-read it often. I highly recommend it to all ages." – Ferrin Brandon, Amazon Reviewer

Not Cinderella's Type

by Jenni James

Jenni James

This book is dedicated to Parnel and Sylvie Bennetts. May you continue to shine and soar in all you do.

Jenni James

Chapter 1

"Indy! Come on—let's go."

I groaned as I rolled over on the grass. This so wasn't my life. Why did PE have to be so hard, anyway? Was the coach's goal to kill everyone who was seriously PE challenged? I needed an excuse card or something. Like one of those "get out of jail free" cards. In fourth grade, my friend Gabby Mineyard had one from her doctor because of some fictitious disease. Okay, so it probably wasn't fictitious, but I swear she was completely normal and could do anything at all during the summer—anything. Like ride a bike, go swimming, climb trees—anything. Until school started. Then there was that glorious "exempt from PE" card again.

"Indy!"

Maxton was still yelling at me. Couldn't he see I was in pain? As in, suffering here? Whatever—it didn't matter. Ms. Bullington was going to come back around the Flagstaff High School track with the other runners any minute and chew me out anyway. Time to suck it up.

I groaned again for good measure and rolled over onto my knees. I took the hand offered me and got up. I was about to thank Maxton for being there, but to my knowledge, Maxton's chest wasn't quite so large, and he wasn't so tall, either. I jerked my head up and came face-to-face with the hottest junior in school, Bryant Bailey.

"What?" I asked, not willing to give him an inch this time. "Why are you here?"

A playful grin spread across his face. "Why are you so mean to me?"

I glared over his shoulder at Maxton for not telling me Bryant was there. He just shrugged back.

Then I turned my glare to Bryant. "You need to come with a warning label or something so people can be prepared when you show up." I pushed past him and grabbed my water bottle. It didn't matter if Ms. Bullington was angry at me or not, there was no way I was sticking around PE another minute. Lamely—literally—I began to limp off the grass, across the track field, and toward the building behind the bleachers. Dang my stupid foot, anyway. I was always twisting my ankle when I tried to run. Always.

Some people were born with grace, and others were meant to watch graceful people from far away. Like miles away. It wasn't hard to guess which category of people I fit into.

Bryant followed me. *Of course.* "Are you really going to blow me off?"

I tried to whirl around, but I forgot about my foot. However, my foot didn't forget it was twisted, and it reminded me—sharply. "Yeesh!" I headed straight. Apparently, walking forward was better than turning around. "Do you expect anything else, Bryant? Seriously? I could so kill you right now, and you know it. In fact, I'm pretty sure that in seventeen states, it'd be legal to kill you. Most people would call it self-defense."

He rolled his eyes, but matched his super-long stride to my shorter one. "You can run away all you want. I'm still going to make it up to you one day."

"No, you're not. I don't want you to. The best way to make anything up is just to leave me alone. Please."

"Do you really despise me that much?"

"Yes."

"Liar."

Urgh. What was I going to have to do to get this guy off my back? I stopped. "If you want to make it up to me, go away. I'm fine. I need some time alone to process it, not to be reminded every five seconds."

"But I've apologized a hundred times. I had no idea it was there. I didn't see it. It was an accident. And every time I see you, I feel awful. I don't even know what to do. I'm not some weird, awful guy—you've gotta give me a chance and let me make it up to you!"

All at once, my heart was heavy and my foot hurt and my chest felt like the Hulk was squeezing it and I wanted out of this dang school. Away from Bryant Bailey and everyone else who had ruined everything special in my life. I just wanted not to remember terrible things. Was that so hard? Except, every time I turned around, there was Bryant again—caught up in his own psycho-codependency or something where he wanted everyone to like him and everything to be fine. But you know what? I wasn't going to like him. Not now, not ever. And it was never going to get better.

So he needed to deal with it somewhere else. What's done was done, and that's that. Showing up all the time, trying to make me feel happy or something was certainly not going to fix anything.

I opened the outside door to the gym and limped inside.

"Cindy, please…"

This time, I did whirl around just as he came into the building. Ouch. "Cindy?" How did he know my real name? My mom's name. No one knew that name. Not even Maxton, and he knew me back when my mom was still alive.

Bryant must've taken my facing him as a good sign because in the next second, he was holding my arm and looking at me seriously. "Will you forgive me?"

Didn't he hear a word I just said? I lost it. In retrospect, I probably shouldn't have, but I was done. Yeah, I was a little mean, but this guy was getting borderline stalkerish, and enough was enough. As in, I was completely and totally through with being reminded of everything that'd gone wrong in my life. And calling me Cindy was the last straw.

I tugged my arm away. "No, Bryant. I won't forgive you for killing my cat! That cat was from my mom. The last gift I'd gotten from her before she died in a car accident. It just so happens that I was named after my mom, and until now, she was the only person who ever called me Cindy."

His eyes widened in shock, and his mouth opened slightly. Thankfully, he didn't speak, or I might've punched him.

"Now, if you will kindly leave me alone to mourn the loss of the last gift I was ever given, who was one of my best friends—and no! I don't expect you to know anything about how awesome cats are, okay?—but she was, and now she's gone. Because you had to speed around by my street and—"

He pulled me in for a big hug. "I'm sorry, Indy. I'm so, so sorry."

"And then to top it all off, you come out with Cindy? Why? *How*?" I tried to push away, but his arms were wrapped around me too tightly. "You know what—I don't want to know. All I care about is when this pain will stop. When will I be able to think about happy things again and just be normal?"

He said it before I could. "Never. You'll never be the same again."

"No." I sniffed. And that's when I realized why he was hugging me so tight. "Dang it. I'm crying?" I pulled away this time, and he let me go. Yep, the whole front of his shirt was wet.

Bryant Bailey made me cry. My sophomore year of high school. I hadn't cried since my mom died. Not when I had to move into my aunt and uncle's house and live in their creepy basement room, not when my cousins made fun of me and told me how ugly I was. And I didn't cry when I became their stupid servant, when my aunt left me with all the chores since my cousins were too involved in after-school activities to have time to clean. And I didn't even cry when Mrs. Wiggins, my cat died—I was too angry to cry. Yet, now here I was, standing in the school gym and crying in front of the one guy I detested most.

And then I said it—the most immature words that have ever left my mouth. "I hate you." I cringed as soon as I said them, but they were out and they were the truth, so I looked up at him . . . and saw Bryant for possibly the first time in my life. Really saw him.

His dark eyes searched mine, long and hard, as if they were prying out every single one of my secrets. This tall, extremely good-looking dark-haired prince-type guy just stared at me. He should've been chasing the pretty girls at school, or working out in the weight room, or writing some amazing symphony that would make him incredibly famous, but instead, he was standing there with me. Then those worried brows of his came together and his mouth turned down a little and he spoke the words that honestly broke me. I have no idea why—but later in my creepy basement room all alone, I sobbed and sobbed and sobbed. For the first time in years, I let everything out.

"I hate me too," he whispered.

And then he kissed me on the cheek, whispered "Sorry" in my ear, and then left.

Chapter 2

"Indy, get up!"

I rolled over in bed and attempted not to groan out loud. I felt like I'd been hit by a semi-truck. And my pounding head wasn't helping.

"Indy! What's taking you so long? Get up here now!" Aunt Clarise was in a mood today.

Sitting up, I moved my matted hair off my face and then rubbed my eyes until I could see the alarm clock. Nine twenty. *No!* I never slept in that late on Saturdays! I jumped up and then winced when the pain in my head bounced around my skull. Good grief. Slowly, I lay back down and brought the covers over my head.

I hated crying hangovers. I'd totally forgotten what they felt like until that moment, but they were bad. It was like you'd literally cried out every single tear in your body until you'd dehydrated yourself or something—I didn't know. I just knew my headache was the stuff nightmares were made of.

"Indy! If you don't get your butt up here this second, you'll be grounded again!"

Wasn't I already grounded? I took a few deep breaths and attempted to think straight. My pillow was soft, the covers were warm, my cat was dead, and I couldn't care less about chores right now. I just couldn't.

When I heard Clarise's feet pounding down the stairs, I admit, I kind of freaked. My heart clenched, and I burrowed deeper into the covers. Perhaps if I pretended to be asleep…

"Indy Ella Zimmerman, you will get up this instant and go upstairs. Have you seen the state of this house? Did you do anything last night? Anything at all? Because I can tell you right now—nothing was done! Our dinner dishes are still on the table. There's food all over the place, and pots and pans. That floor hasn't been swept or mopped, and we're not even going to talk about the living room right now. It's a disaster! Clothes, shoes, papers—everywhere!"

She whipped the covers off me, and a whoosh of cold air invaded my happy place. I attempted to blink awake for real now, but her shouting only increased the pounding in my head. Everything hurt so much.

"What's wrong with you?" I could tell she was close to losing it. "You'd better not be sick! I don't have time for you to be sick today! I've got people coming over at noon, remember? For my presentation. This house better look marvelous. Do you understand? I will take away every privilege you have if you just lie there and pretend to be sick."

"Fine," I mumbled as I tried to sit up again. I actually made it upright and even opened my eyes, but the heaviness inside—that intense need to lie back down—took over, and I slumped back into bed. "I'll do it before twelve." I could hear the slurring in my words. "I promise. I'm not feeling good right now."

Clarise stood there and tapped on the dresser, her long fingernails tick-ticking on the green wooden surface. I wasn't sure what she was debating, but she finally said,

"You look awful too. You didn't come up for dinner last night. Maybe I don't want you touching our dishes until you feel better—I don't want whatever disease you're spreading. Especially since I'm doing a presentation on healthy essential oils."

I held my breath. I'd never known her to actually give me a break. She was usually positive I was lying about something and never believed a word I said. In an odd, almost motherly moment, I felt the bedspread flip back over me before Clarise went upstairs. It was strangely soothing and nice. As if . . . as if . . . urgh. Everything hurt too much to try to find a suitable analogy. There wasn't one.

I was her younger sister's daughter. The younger sister she never got along with. The one who was—as Clarise would put it—"too lazy to ever be human, or likeable." Apparently, I looked just like my mom, and Clarise was stuck with me and—until recently—the dreaded cat, too. My dad left when my mom was still pregnant with me, and I never met him. Mom got divorced before she was even showing. To this day, all I have is a name, Ryan Alysop, the guy she was married to for less than a year.

Mom never really dated anyone after that—I think he sort of broke her. Instead, she went to work full time, doing everything she could to support us both. Even though Mom was successful, she had a lot of past debts my dad had left behind, including a car that had been in her name that he took too. The cops never found that car, and Mom still had to make the payments.

It wasn't exactly easy for her, though I learned most of this from my aunt and grandma after Mom died—she'd always kept the worst parts hidden from me. Sometimes late at night when I try to imagine what she must've gone through—single, alone, heartbroken, scared, with several bills and a tiny baby to look after—I can't breathe. I never saw that side. Maybe my mom wasn't human—maybe Clarise was right—but I grew up knowing I was a princess. That I was loved and cared for. Mom taught me about helping others and sharing what I have with friends and always, always to smile through trials. She tried so hard to instill all of that, and for a while, I was her Cindy Ella, or her happy Cinderella princess, as she used to call me. My life was poofy pink dresses and sunshine and balloons and blissful walks and feeding ducks at the park—all of it. I was loved, secure, and cheerful. My life was a fairy tale, and I was the star.

Everything was so good.

And then she was gone.

One stupid, ugly car accident when I was ten, and my beautiful, courageous mother was gone. And in that split second, my bright world turned black, and everything I thought I knew changed in an instant. Aunt Clarise was so grief-stricken and angry, all she did was berate my mom. I'd hear her chewing out her dead sister for hours. It was like everything she ever wanted to say came out. In full force. I'd like to believe Clarise didn't know I could hear her, that when she drank too much and spoke too loudly, she thought I was fast asleep downstairs. But I wasn't. I heard everything she said.

I couldn't sleep for weeks after Mom had gone. I cried and cried and cried. It messed me up more than I was willing to admit, and honestly, I didn't know if I'd ever fully recover.

When I woke up again, it was after one, and I was starving. I could hear the muffled sounds of my aunt's voice and women laughing. Her presentation was still going on, and she'd be ticked if I showed my haggard face anywhere near her friends.

I rolled onto my back, brought the covers up under my chin, and looked around the sparse room. When I first moved there, in an attempt to be generous, Clarise had said I could decorate it any way I wanted to so it would feel like home.

But I was ten, it didn't feel like home, and I was too sad to attempt to decorate anything. I didn't even know what I'd want to do with it. It had been so long since the offer, I was too afraid to ask if I could still change it up.

It'd been used as a storage room, so it was the afterthought of the large home. The walls were white—though with the small basement window above my bed, they looked more gray than anything. There never was adequate sunlight, which was fine with me—it sort of suited my mood. I had brought very little from my house. Everything we had—dolls and all—was sold to pay for the funeral and other expenses.

The creepiest part were the pipes that ran along the side of the ceiling. They tended to make strange sounds at unexpected times during the day and night, though I didn't realize what was making the sounds at first. It took a couple of years before I pinpointed the pipes. Now the odd banging or rushing of water only startled me when I was thinking too much.

My throat was dry, and my stomach grumbled. Dang. I was hungry. I figured it'd been at least twenty-four hours since I last ate. Cautiously, I climbed out of bed, and was surprised that my pounding headache seemed to have faded a bit after my nap. It was more of a solid, workable headache than the horrid thing it had been. I scrounged around in my backpack, found a half-full water bottle, and guzzled it down. Then I rummaged through my dresser and came up with a sleeve of Ritz crackers I'd stashed there a few weeks ago.

The crackers weren't too bad. I was worried they'd be stale or something, but they were fine. So I ate and hung out in my room, deciding that if I couldn't leave without walking right past the party, I'd better do something productive. After about ten minutes, homework was a no-go. This headache wasn't playing around. I probably needed some Tylenol or something. But again, that was stored in the medicine cabinet, and I'd have to pass by the presentation to get it. I sighed and plopped down on my bed.

Laughter.

Those women could stay up there all afternoon.

I stared at the ceiling, trying to decide if I'd rather sleep off the rest of my headache, but I wasn't really tired anymore.

Then the strangest thing happened. I swore I heard Clarise's voice laughing and chattering as she headed down the stairs.

"Indy loves company! Her room is down here. She likes the peace and quiet away from her cousins upstairs."

Holy cow! Was she bringing some of her friends down here to see me? I quickly grabbed a comb and began hacking at my hair and then threw a sweatshirt on over my PJ top. I flung the bedspread over the messy sheets and chucked a couple of pillows off the floor to land near the headboard. Then I stuffed some clothes back into my drawers that were hanging out.

Clarise knocked and used her sticky-sweet voice. "Indy? Are you there? We've got something that'll cheer you up."

This really was happening. *How* could this be happening? The last thing I wanted was some weird-smelling oils on me. "Yeah, I'm here. Just a second." I scooped up a ton of trash and put it in the can near the door.

"How are you feeling?" she called through the door.

"Great. A lot better now that I've slept." I zipped up my backpack and shoved it in the far corner, and then tossed my shoes beside the dresser. I quickly glanced around. No embarrassing underwear anywhere. Room looked pretty decent. My head was definitely pounding again.

I pasted a smile on my face as I opened the door. "Hi." And then that smile dropped. "What in the world are you doing here?"

Chapter 3

Bryant looked over at Clarise and then gave a nervous laugh. He opened his mouth to say something, but my aunt beat him to it.

"Look who came by!" she gushed. "That guy who hit your cat. He wants to apologize, and has a present for you. Isn't he so sweet?"

"Very." It took every bit of self-control not to glare at him as I moved back and let him in the room.

"Well, you two have fun. I still have some guests over." She went to turn back down the hall. "Oh, and Indy, I can't wait to hear all about it."

"Okay." Nice. I shut the door and looked at him.

"Hey," he said.

"Hey."

All at once, I felt incredibly uncomfortable with Bryant Bailey in my bedroom. He was way too tall for this little space and made the whole place shrink. Before I died of claustrophobia, I opened the door and left it wide open. "So why are you really here?" I asked.

He took a deep breath. "I knew you'd say no, so I came without asking."

"Caught that. So what do you want?"

"I'd like us to be friends."

I blinked. Was this some sort of joke or something? "What?"

"I want to get to know you. Be your friend."

"No." I walked out of the room and down the hall to the cold, unused den. At least it was a bigger space than my tiny, creepy bedroom. The den had a couple of brown leather couches and a large TV. It was supposed to be used for football games and movie nights, but everyone else had a TV in their bedroom and a large one in the upstairs family room, so they really didn't get together for much down here. Hence the reason why the den was pretty much always cold.

Bryant followed me. "Look, do you have something against having guy friends?"

"Of course not. Maxton Hoyster is one of my best friends." I plopped down on the smallest couch and put my feet on the other seat so he'd have to take the larger one. "Guys are way easier to get along with than girls."

"So?"

"Bryant, you're only being my friend out of pity. No one wants a pity friend—or a pity date, for that matter. We'd all like to have stuff in our lives that's genuine."

"Who said anything about a date? Besides, I'm genuinely worried about you. Is that a start?"

I rolled my eyes and sat back. "You're not worried about me any more than my aunt and uncle are. You don't know me well enough to be worried about me." I paused. "What's in that bag? It smells good."

"This?" He dangled it out with a long arm. "I brought you a peace offering."

"Food?" I scooted forward.

"Captain Jack's famous burger."

"You're kidding." My mouth was already watering.

"And fries." He grinned. "See? I knew I could get on your good side eventually."

"You have no idea. I'm starving!"

Without another word, he handed the whole bag over to me. Inside were two burgers and two packages of fries. Still warm. "You will be blessed by the gods for this." I pulled out one of each and tossed him back the bag.

"Are you sure you don't want more? The way you're digging in to that burger, I have no problem giving you mine too."

For the first time in a long time, I laughed. It was around a bite of food, but I laughed anyway. After I'd calmed my ravenous appetite and began to eat like a normal human being again, I asked, "So, how did you know I'd be hungry?"

"Because I'd spent a good chunk of my morning lying in bed feeling sorry for myself and thinking about you, and when I realized I was hungry, I figured you were probably hungry too. It was a simple math equation, really." He grinned a devastatingly handsome grin and leaned back on the couch, holding the rest of his burger. "I have three sisters, and I know that when they get upset, they live in their rooms. And then once they finally emerge the next day, they've turned into ornery wolves desperate to eat anything they can get their hands on." He took a bite. "So one plus one equals two. I knew if I was hungry, chances were you'd be too."

I stared at him for a long time before I said anything. I honestly didn't want to trust Bryant. I didn't want to be his friend, either—or anything else, for that matter. Not that there'd be anything else—I just didn't understand him, I guess. After the last of my fries were gone, I asked, "So why me? Why have you decided to stalk me?"

His eyebrows jumped up. "You think I stalk you? Like I'm a crazy stalker-person?"

Well, if the shoe fits … I didn't say anything, and eventually, he nodded.

"Okay, I guess I can see why you'd find me a little odd."

"Ha. I wish you were odd. Odd, I could handle."

He smirked. "Fine. Scary, then. From your perspective, I guess I can see why."

"Okay, but why are you here? You didn't answer that."

He finished off his burger, tossed his empty wrapper in the brown bag, and then chucked it over to me to do the same. "I don't know why. Beyond feeling bad about—er, hitting your cat."

"The word is *murder*. You murdered my cat."

He smiled ruefully. "All right. Beyond feeling bad about murdering your cat, I don't know why I'm here." Shrugging, he continued, "I know I need to be. Something about you . . . about this . . . I'm not done. I should be here, be next to you, so I am."

What in the world? "You say that like you're part of some disturbing psychic movie or something."

"It's not psychic—it's just a feeling. You need me. Or maybe I need you—something here clicks, and it hasn't ever clicked with other people before."

"Right. Now I'm just terrified. You can leave anytime."

He leaned forward and put his elbows on his knees. "Indy, stop. You know I'm not a psycho. I figured you're the type of girl who wants the plain truth, no sugar coating, just what it is. So I'm here. Telling you the truth. I don't know . . . I only know I feel better talking to you."

"Ugh. Bryant, this has nothing to do with me. If you need to come over here to feel better about killing my cat, fine. You can placate yourself and show up, I guess. But to say this is for me too—that's where I call you on it. If this was about me, you'd walk away and leave me alone."

Those dark eyes bore into mine, and for an instant, I could hardly breathe. What was it about this guy that was so fascinating, anyway? Something about him, about his stupid need to be here, was oddly intriguing.

"Indy, you're wrong. You think you've got the whole world sorted into little boxes, and when someone steps out of their box and does something you aren't expecting, you try your hardest to push them back in. Well, I don't fit. I'm not *meant* to fit. Your walls are high and thick, but I'll get through them somehow. Wait and see."

A flash of irritation swept through me. "So much for thinking we were getting somewhere. When are you leaving again?" I pretended to look at a watch I most definitely didn't have on. "Now?"

Bryant stood up, and for a second, my heart dropped. I didn't know why, but I didn't want him to go. I shoved the feeling down and stood too. "Well, thanks for the lunch. You rock." My attempt at a thank you was awkwardly lame, but I said the right words, and that had to count for something. I couldn't even look him in the eye as I started to walk out of the room.

"Indy, what are you doing?"

I turned back. "Showing you the door."

One corner of his mouth rose up in this semi-adorable grin. "I'm not going anywhere."

"What? But you stood up."

"Yeah. I thought I'd change it up a little. You're not getting rid of me that easily."

"But . . .?" I didn't know whether to be annoyed or relieved.

"So, I found something out the other day."

I blinked, not sure where he was headed with this. "Okay?"

"It's kind of important. Do you want to go somewhere else to talk? Go get ice cream? Maybe a walk in the park? A drive somewhere?"

"I—" I think my jaw might have hit the ground. Bryant wanted to take me someplace to talk. Was that his way of asking me out on a date? My aunt would lose her mind, especially after that morning. "I really don't think I can."

He sighed. "Look, Indy. I'm not trying to make things weird here. But I'm serious. My dad told me something, and I'd like to talk to you about it."

"Okay. Aside from the fact that you're totally weird and I don't trust you and all that, I really mean I don't think I can. As in, I'm not sure I'm allowed to leave this house with you. My aunt is . . . uh . . . things are . . . well, anyway. I don't think I could leave. But I'm curious. What did your dad have to say?" I walked back over and sat down on the couch. This time, he came and sat right next to me. I should've kicked him out when I had the chance. Dang it.

Bryant leaned back, probably because I was acting like a dork, but I didn't care. I preferred to have my own personal space.

"So, you were saying?" I folded my arms.

"This is going to be unusual, so give me a second to explain."

I laughed again. I couldn't help it. "Bryant, nothing about you is usual."

"Yeah, well, okay. I'm just going to jump in there and say it." His dark eyes looked right into mine. "So, about five years ago, my dad came home from work really late. There was a car accident. He'd been the car behind her when she was hit by a truck and then swerved into oncoming traffic and was hit again by a semi."

Oh, my gosh. I put my hands to my mouth. "Stop."

"No. Let me finish. Please."

I closed my eyes and promised myself I wouldn't cry. "Okay." My voice barely came out as a whisper.

"He was the one to call 911. Then he stopped traffic and rushed to her. My dad never said how bad it was, only that she was dying, and he knew she would never make it to the hospital. So while the ambulance came and the firefighters and the cops and everything, he held her hand. And she said something."

"Mom." I began to cry. I couldn't help it. I was grateful someone was there for her, but so mad it wasn't me.

"She said, 'Please tell Cindy I love her. Tell my Indy that she is and will always be a princess. Tell her that no matter what I'll be with her—I wouldn't leave her. She'll be scared that I've left her like her dad. Tell her I'm there.'

"She held on to my dad's hands and asked him to give you the message. When I finally confessed to my dad the other day that I'd hit a girl's cat and she went to school with me and her name was Indy, he told me the rest and asked me to come see you."

I wiped at my face. "So that's how you knew my name was Cindy?"

Bryant nodded, his own eyes wet. "My dad told me, because your mom told him. You're Cinderella."

Chapter 4

If I'd have been standing, I would've fallen down. "How long did your dad talk to my mom before she died?" What else had she told him?

"I asked him the same question." Bryant shook his head. "Like fifteen, maybe twenty minutes." He plucked at the leather on the couch. "They talked a lot. My dad was trying everything to keep her awake and focused on him instead of the pain. He said he could tell what a good woman she was—and more importantly, how much she loved her daughter. She didn't dwell on anything negative, but just focused on how grateful she was to have you. And how you gave her the will and strength and drive to go on."

I wiped at more tears. My headache was never going to go away. I was sure of it. Not after today.

Bryant still didn't look up at me. "My dad kind of rambled. It was like these memories of your mom's death came back to him. He said she was beautiful. Even with the mess of the car wreck, he could still tell she was beautiful."

"She was," I whispered.

"She loved you."

"She did. If I knew anything in my life, I knew I was loved. Cherished."

He nodded, and then wiped his eyes some more. "I'm sorry, Indy."

I took a deep breath and let it out slowly. "Well, junk happens to everyone, right? It's what life is all about. Bad things happening to people."

"Well, yeah, I guess. That's part of it, but you didn't mention the other part."

This time, our gazes locked. "And what's that?"

"Life isn't only about the trials. It's about how you overcome them."

I flinched slightly and tried to look away, but couldn't. Something about his words ripped through me in a way I hadn't been pierced before. "What do you mean?"

Bryant tilted his head as he looked at me. He was seriously good at long, soul-searching stares. It was like being hypnotized.

"What?" I asked as I attempted to break the spell he had over me.

"Trials don't stop—they never will. It's how you learn from them, grow from them, and help others learn and grow too that defines you as a person."

I still had no idea what he meant.

"You could choose to stay here hidden away and hate life, or you can choose to move forward and help others heal. To reach out in the community and become something to someone else. You're not alone. People die every day. It's kind of inevitable. However, you could help and grow from what happened to promising others can move on too."

I was feeling a little out of my element and kind of annoyed. "So, are you saying I'm lost here?"

"I'd say you're pretty angry at life right now. I don't know who that girl is that my dad learned about five years ago—that one your mom told him about. I don't see her."

"It's because she's dead! She died when my mom died." Suddenly, I'd had enough of Bryant Bailey. "You can go now, all right? Just leave." I stood up. I'd heard all I was willing to. I was sick of his prying and meddling and making all the pain come back. What was he, anyway? "You're a kid like me, Bryant. I'm sixteen—you're probably seventeen. You're not some therapist—you're just a guy who's decided all this stuff and thinks you can help me. Well, you can't. So just go."

"Indy, wait." He stood up. "I know this is hard to take in all at once, with my dad's story and all that. I know. I'm sorry. I can slow down. I only wanted to help. That's all."

"I don't need it. Can't you see that? I'm perfectly fine on my own. In fact, if it wasn't for you, I wouldn't be a crying mess anyway. Just go away and leave me alone."

"All my instincts say stay right here."

"Your instincts need to get a reality check. This isn't about you—it's about me. I've been saying the same thing, and you're not listening."

"If I leave now, I may never get this close again."

What in the—"Oh, yes, you're right. We're done. This closeness thing you're trying to create is so over. That was ruined about three minutes ago when you were trying to evaluate my life. *My life.* Okay? It's *mine.* Get that through your head." I picked up an accent pillow and debated throwing it at his stubborn skull. "You know what I need? I need to breathe and walk and get through high school and qualify for some college somewhere so I can get a real job and get myself out of this house and on my own where I can do whatever I want, whenever I want, without anyone else telling me things I don't want to hear."

"It sounds like an awesome plan. I'd do that."

Urgh! I wanted to shove him across the room. No one had ever irritated me as much as this guy. "Just what are you trying to save me from, Bryant? What makes you so certain I need saving?"

"Whoa. I didn't say anything about saving anyone—I'm only trying to help."

Gah. "Stop. Seriously, stop. There's nothing, absolutely nothing you can say right now that will make this better."

"Every situation is different," he said quietly, still standing there strong and firm and immovable. I didn't know whether to laugh or cry at his stubbornness. "But believe it or not, I can relate. I know what you're going through. And your anger is completely justified."

"Really?" I put my hands on my hips.

He nodded and looked away. "My mom died when I was ten too. Almost a year before yours did."

What? I sat down. All at once, everything stopped.

A strange humming feeling came over me. It was intense and strong, and like I wasn't really connecting with my body—or more importantly, like every fiber of my being was waiting and willing to understand what had just happened.

He talked quietly and slowly. "I know that rage. I know that lost feeling. I know that shock. I just don't want you to think you need to kill yourself too."

My head jerked up. *How did he know?* I blinked and then blinked again. And if I thought I'd cried before, this was an all-new gut-wrenching experience. This time, I cried for the guy across from me. The happy guy at school. The guy everyone knew and loved. The guy the girls stupidly swooned over. He had a secret. He had my secret. *He had wanted to die too.* And that moment connected us for the first time.

Chapter 5

I felt as though cement had smashed against my chest. Everything was tight, and I could barely breathe. Also, a part of me felt like an idiot for chewing him out. For believing my life was more important than his—that I had experienced worse. Bryant was right—junk happens to everyone. I wanted to say something. To talk normally instead of like some raving lunatic.

I started with the obvious. "Sorry."

He attempted a laugh and then said, "Don't be. I was angry for years too. My dad has stepped up to the plate and become better at the family thing, but yeah, it was my mom who could do that."

I looked around the sparsely decorated room and whispered, "Don't tell my aunt, but yeah, my mom was much better at it too."

He bit his lip to hide a grin. "Not very motherly?"

"No. Not at all." It felt good to share with someone. "Let's just say she's more the type to make magnanimous gestures and expect everything to be okay after that."

"Don't you have cousins? Two of them, if I remember." He glanced toward the hall that led up to the stairs. "Isn't this where Jayda and Kaitlyn live?"

So he knew them. Of course he knew them. Everybody did. "Yep."

"Jayda's a junior with me and Kaitlyn's a sophomore with you, right? Or did I get the two confused? Sometimes I do that."

"No, you're right."

"And they pretty much leave you alone down here?"

I shrugged. "Well, you know basements. They're not usually the main hangout spot."

His eyebrows came together, and he looked a bit confused. "I thought this house was huge. Aren't there more rooms upstairs?"

A sharp pain ripped through the cement on my chest, but I tried to pretend like it was no big deal. "Yep. There are six bedrooms upstairs, then the main floor with two more guest rooms, a kitchen, dining room, music room-slash-library, and large family room. And then there's the basement, shared with the four-car garage and woodshop. There's this den room here, small bathroom, and a few rooms for storage. My room had a bunch of Rubbermaid totes, and they pulled those out and took them all somewhere else before I came here."

He sat down and rested his knees on his elbows. "Okay. So let me get this straight. This house has eight actual bedrooms?"

"No! I mean, yeah, but the girls had one turned into a playroom years ago, and there are two offices up there. For my aunt's essential oil business, and then my uncle's home office."

"And then two guest rooms on the main floor?"

"Oh, nobody goes into those. And they need them. Clarise is always hosting someone. Family, friends—people are always here."

He nodded and then sort of grunted or disgust-sighed or something. I have no idea what that sound was—it was all male. "So let me get this straight. You're ten years old, your cousins are the same age and have this room upstairs full of toys and their stuff, so full that they don't have any extra space in their own rooms for their things, and your mom dies and they're your family and they move you into an old storage room? Why not put you in the toy room?"

My chest clenched tighter. Why was he making this seem so bad? "I really didn't notice. It was their stuff, not mine. I wouldn't have felt comfortable in a room with their things. You know what I mean? Besides, there wasn't really a spot for a bed up there with the dollhouse and built-in shelves and art center. It definitely was a play room."

Bryant got up and began walking down the hall. I thought he was leaving until he opened my bedroom door.

"Hey!" I quickly followed him, but he didn't go inside. He just looked around.

"I know—I'm nosy."

Now I was completely embarrassed about the clutter. "What are you doing?"

He must've seen what he needed to because he shut the door and faced me, those eyes of his doing their magic again.

"What? Yeah, I know. I should probably clean it more, but I was tired last night, and I—"

He lifted his finger under my chin, and I stopped talking. All at once, my heavy chest warmed and lightened completely. In fact, I was pretty sure my heart was beating on overdrive.

"Indy?"

"Yeah?"

"I have one more prying question to ask, and then I promise I'll be good for like twenty minutes or so."

I grinned. "Only twenty?"

"Hey, I try not to make promises I can't keep. You interest me. I can't help myself. So I ask everything I shouldn't."

His finger was warm against my chin, and those eyes glittered in the darker light of the hallway. "Your question?"

"Where are your dolls and stuff?"

What? "My dolls? What are you talking about? Why would I need dolls?"

"You know, from when you were younger. Your cousins had so many toys, they needed another room for them. Where are yours?"

My smile dropped, and I shrugged. "I didn't ever have as many as they did. Mom was more into experiences than things."

"Okay, but you were ten. I expect to see at least a teddy bear, or something on your bed. Or is he hidden away in your closet?"

"The funeral expenses were too high."

His voice came out slow and steady, and that gaze—good grief, his eyes should be illegal. "So they sold everything?"

"Yeah, well, everything but the cat."

His gaze was gone. His lids shut him out just like that. "Wow."

All at once, I felt vulnerable and alone in a darkened hallway with a tall guy I barely knew. Each breath was a completely unique experience. Some came fast, some slow, some skipped altogether.

And then his gaze was back. "I won't ask you to forgive me about Mrs. Wiggins anymore. I'm not even going to expect it."

"I . . . okay." What was I supposed to say?

His finger started to lift my chin a bit higher, and his gaze shifted to my lips. Holy cow! Was he actually going to kiss me? My eyes flew to his mouth, and I wondered what it'd feel like. My breathing, my heartbeats—everything rested on this moment.

"Indy?"

"Uh-huh?"

"I really, really want to kiss you right now. And I know you're going to say no, so I'm not going to invade and do anything that will ruin this—"

I'd heard enough. I stepped up on tiptoe and kissed him instead.

And my word! I had no idea a girl could melt from a kiss.

But I did.

Totally. And completely. Melted.

And you know what? I didn't regret one bit of it. I should've, but I didn't. And it was amazing.

When Bryant pulled back, his adorable face was in complete shock. "So, am I forgiven?"

After a few breaths to calm myself, I tried act chill. "Never."

He gave a half grin and then said, "Thank you."

"For?"

He was nervous. I could tell he was nervous and didn't quite know what to do. "Kissing me."

Do guys usually go around thanking people for kissing them? He was so funny.

"I mean . . . I meant, thanks for not punching me in the face."

"That's for later."

"Oh."

We were still standing in the middle of the hall, and I knew something was supposed to happen, but I didn't know what. I was curious enough about him to want him to stay. Then all of a sudden, I blurted out the next thing I thought of. "So, how did your mom die?"

"This is about me now?"

"I figured it was time."

He hesitated and looked between my bedroom door and the hall. "Do you want to go somewhere and chat, or is right here okay?"

I almost slid right down the wall and talked to him there in the hallway because I was weird like that, but then I remembered that sometimes voices carried up from that spot, so I motioned him toward the den again.

"I think this is becoming my new favorite area." He crashed onto the large couch and then patted the seat next to him.

Everything became odd, and I wasn't sure what to do. So, we'd kissed, but now what? Were we supposed to be all cuddly or something? Or would stuff go back to normal? Gah. I really wasn't good with this whole relationship thing. Not that we were in one—I guess I didn't know how to get in one if I wanted to, or what the rules were.

I sat next to him, but maintained a safe distance. Meaning, I practically hugged the opposite arm from where he was sitting. Then I put a pillow between us for good measure. "So how did your mom die?" I asked again, once I thought my voice wouldn't betray my nervousness.

"Nothing typical, like cancer or something. It was sudden, like your mom. One minute, she was riding her bike to work, and the next, she was hit by a guy who'd been texting and didn't see her. And that was it. She was gone. And everything in my life changed. I . . . I don't know why it happened. I asked myself that a lot at first. Was there anything she could've done differently?"

He took a deep breath. "That sort of thinking drives you crazy. What I do know is that one day, we were this happy family with four kids, and then the next, my dad was a frazzled widower with four kids. My oldest sister, MacKenzie, was fourteen when it happened. She completely lost it. I still don't think she's gotten over it. Then there was me and my two little sisters, who were eight and six at the time.

"MacKenzie took over and began cooking and helping us with homework until my dad could get home. It was a hard time for everyone. We fought a lot and stressed out more and honestly, I can't remember most of it. I hid in my room and locked the door and slept a lot."

I could relate. "The last thing I wanted to do after my mom died was act normal. I spent a lot of time in my room staring at the walls, snuggling Mrs. Wiggins and crying."

He winced, but I was grateful he didn't apologize again. I hadn't even realized I'd brought up the cat until he reacted. "So that's why it didn't bother you when you moved into this basement?"

"What didn't bother me?"

"The fact your aunt and uncle treated you differently."

"No. I didn't think about it. I've always felt so alone and not part of their world, it never dawned on me to feel any other way. I'll always be the intruder."

"Indy. Don't say that."

Enough about me. "So, when did you want to die?"

Chapter 6

He sort of gasped. "Wow. When you want to know something, you have no problem jumping in there."

"I learned from the best."

"A direct hit. I acknowledge." He rose an eyebrow and grinned. "Right. So, when did I want to die? Well, almost immediately, I guess. I missed my mom like crazy. She was my best friend, but I didn't know it until she was gone. We were really close." He picked up the pillow in between us and tossed it on the floor.

I almost protested, but listened instead.

"She was riding her bike because we were going to enter a parent/kid triathlon that summer. I really, really wanted to try it out and do it, but Dad was too busy. So one day, Mom saw that I was bummed and pulled out her old bike and helmet and we went for our first ride. That turned into a nightly thing right before dinner. Then every morning, she'd wake me up at five to head to the gym's swimming pool. She was a beast."

"Wow, she was serious about training."

"Yeah. Mom had a competitive streak. If she was going to do something, she sure as fire wanted to give it a real shot." He was silent for a minute and then said, "We'd run, too. Every weekend, she'd talk me out running. It was hard, but it was fun too. And then it was gone."

"Did you still do the triathlon?"

"By myself? No. That day, I curled up under my covers and never got out of bed. I don't even think Dad realized what was going on—none of them did. They'd pretty much forgotten all about the race and what day it was and all that. But I hadn't. That's the day I really cried."

"I'm sorry."

I could see the tears forming in his eyes again, and it was making me nearly lose it. "The worst part was, I knew she was there. Like, in my room with me. And I missed her so much, it hurt. I could feel her wrapping me up in the covers, almost like she was holding me while I cried. I knew then that she missed me too and wasn't going to leave me alone. It was so warm in that room, but it wasn't the same, and we both knew it."

I thought of all the different times I was sure I'd felt my mom throughout my life, and I cried with him. "It's weird to explain, isn't it? It's like they're there. But you know they're not really. But it's so good to know they think about you. It's so comforting and painful at the same time."

"Dad calls it bittersweet."

I nodded. "That'd be a good word for it."

"Anyway, Mom probably saved my life that day. Not that I knew how to kill myself exactly, or would've had the guts, but that moment—when I knew she was holding me—has stopped me more than anything the older I've gotten."

"Like on her birthday, or the anniversary of her death? When it just gets too hard to handle?" Those were the worst.

"Yep. On days like that, when all you want is to be with her again. And really talk to her and laugh and tease and all of that. That's when it haunts you the most. The need to go too."

His words hit home. I had other days, too, when things would go really wrong, but for the most part, that was exactly what it was like for me.

"Wow. Nothing like bringing in the heavy." He rubbed his face. "Sorry. I really don't go places and act intense like this all the time."

I wondered what he was like under normal circumstances. Like on a soccer field or something, just goofing around. I was about to change the subject and ask him something fun when Jayda came down the stairs and knocked on my bedroom door.

"Hey, Indy. Is Bryant Bailey in there? Mom said he came to the house like an hour ago."

I could see her from down the hall, and Bryant and I shared a look. It wasn't like we could hide forever though. "We're over here," I called.

Jayda started. I could tell she was embarrassed, but she recovered quickly enough as she came down the hall, all smiles. "Hey, so you are here!"

"Yep." Bryant smiled back.

There was a moment of nearly attempted musical chairs. Jayda wanted to sit on the couch with us, but didn't know how. I wasn't about to move and I think she realized that, so she sat across from us instead. Then she promptly ignored me.

"So, Bryant, what brings you here? How are you doing?" She flipped her long, perfectly curled hair over her shoulder.

"I'm good." He looked back at me. "Indy and I were swapping stories."

"Ooh!" She grinned. "I like stories. What stories where you sharing?"

"About death," I interjected, wanting to give her a little reminder I was there. Then I changed the subject because honestly, it wasn't any of her business. "Is your mom still having her presentation?"

"No. Thankfully, it just ended." She leaned back into the couch and sighed. "Talk about torture."

"What's so torturous?" Bryant asked.

I was about to explain, but Jayda beat me to it.

"When my mom does these essential oil presentations, she has a bunch of women over. First off, the house has to be spotless, with like, all this delicious food. And then she makes us stay in our rooms and not show our faces until the guests are gone."

"You're basically all stuck, huh?" Bryant chuckled. "How long has she been doing these? And how did I get let into the house?"

"I had no idea you were here until Mom told me a few minutes ago." Jayda brought her feet up from the floor and tucked them under her.

I decided to go ahead and answer his questions. "Aunt Clarise has been an essential oils consultant for years. Since before I got here. So these parties are pretty frequent—probably three or four times a week. You must've made an impression on her. Or maybe she didn't want to look bad in front of her clients. Either way, I'm kinda glad you came. This has been fun."

"Talking about death is fun?" Jayda rolled her eyes and then looked at Bryant. "So, what are you doing later tonight? We're having a few friends over to chill and watch some Netflix. Would you like to come?"

It was the first I'd heard anything about a movie night, but Bryant seemed definitely interested. "Sure. I'll have to double-check with my dad, but I don't think I've got anything planned."

Just then, Kaitlyn made it down the stairs. "Jayda, where are you? Mom says Bryant's here."

"He is!" Jayda and Bryant laughed. "Come into the den."

She practically skipped down the hall and had no problem jumping in between me and Bryant. She giggled as she landed on my foot. "Hi, Bryant! How long have you been here?"

Bryant played it cool, but I could tell by the way he scooted back a little that he found her a bit rude. "Indy and I have been getting to know each other the last hour or so. How are you doing?"

"Great!" She giggled again. "So, did Jayda tell you about our Netflix party we're having? You've got to come. It'll be so much fun."

Bryant glanced at me.

"Indy!" Clarise called from upstairs. "Come here. I need you in the kitchen."

My heart dropped. So much for that. I didn't want to tell Bryant that I was heading up for chore duty, or that my cousins probably set this up so they could have him to themselves. Everything was awkward enough as it was. Besides, Bryant Bailey wasn't actually my type—he didn't even fit into my preferred friend parameters—so none of this really mattered anyway. My gorgeous cousins would make him forget I existed in about two more minutes. I plastered on a fake smile. "Hey, that's my aunt. I'll be back in a minute."

"Okay." Bless his heart, he looked concerned for me.

Not that there was anything to be concerned about. I'd known this was coming—it's basically life. I sort of waved, pulled myself out from under Kaitlyn, and headed toward the stairs. By the time I'd reached them, the two girls were talking a hundred miles a minute about their favorite movies. I heard Bryant chuckle as I walked into the kitchen and faced Clarise.

"Hi."

She was ticked. Her high-heeled foot tapped against the large beige tiles of the kitchen floor, and her arms were folded. "Do you have any idea how long my girls and I had to work this morning to get this place looking decent?"

"Sorry." I felt miserable. "Was it hard?"

"You have no idea. And we only had three hours to do it!"

I hated it when she got mad. Her meeting must not have gone as well as planned. "Sorry," I said again. I wasn't sure what else to say.

"You'd better be." She threw her hands in the air and walked into the dining room.

I followed.

"In exchange for living here, you're supposed to do your jobs. And I understand that you were sick. Well, you'd better have been—that look you gave Bryant Bailey when he showed up definitely didn't look sick to me!"

"What look?"

"Don't talk back to me!" Clarise snarled and then pointed to the dining room table. "Get these things packed up and this whole area cleaned immediately. The girls are having their own party tonight, and I want this place looking amazing again."

"Okay."

"That means vacuuming, bathrooms, mopping, dishes … everything! And then you'd better put out some cool junk food snacks too."

Kaitlyn and Jayda were always throwing parties. "Do you have a theme in mind for the platters? Bowls?"

"Not my nice set. Use the normal turquoise stuff. And make sure you get the right napkins this time! They're the ones in the second drawer in the pantry, not the first. The first are for everyday use, and the second are for guests."

"Got it. Anything else?"

"Since you were sick this morning, don't even think about coming to the party tonight."

When had I ever gone to anything my cousins did with their friends? "Not a problem." My heart tightened a bit as the memory of Bryant's shock over the room situation came back full force. It wasn't like any of this was a big deal. It wasn't. They had their life, I had mine, and I think we all preferred it that way.

"Good. That's settled." Clarise began to walk away and then turned. "I'll be back in an hour to see how much you've gotten done. Let's hurry, please?"

In the silence of the kitchen, I could hear laughter coming up from the den, and I quickly prayed that Bryant hadn't heard anything Clarise had said. I mean, it didn't matter, but I . . . he . . . well, he'd been acting weird earlier, and some things I figured were better left secret. Like the cleaning and being in trouble for being sick—a girl's gotta have some pride left. Right?

I began clearing off the dining table, careful not to drop any of the beautiful crystal serving platters. They were laden with bite-sized morsels of gourmet-looking snacks. Clarise usually handed me several printed-off recipes each weekend and I created the presentation menu while she got herself ready for company. She was probably running behind that morning since I never cleaned up from the night before, let alone breakfast this morning, so everyone had to scramble to get it all ready in time. Yeah, I wouldn't be happy at me either for dropping the ball like that.

I took a deep breath and pushed everything out of my mind. My aunt wanted as much done in an hour as possible. And it certainly wasn't impossible to do everything—I would just need to focus and stop the strange pity nonsense that'd briefly taken over my body.

Time to get to work.

Chapter 7

In about forty-five minutes, I'd managed to put away the leftovers, start the dishwasher, clean the bathrooms, vacuum the upstairs and middle floor—I decided to leave the basement alone until Bryant left.—and I swept and mopped the kitchen. By the time Bryant made his way upstairs with my cousins, it looked like I was merely preparing the food for their party.

"Hey, so this is where you went to hide—the kitchen." He grinned and walked over to the counter. "What are you baking in the oven? It smells good."

"They're brownies for tonight," Kaitlyn said. "From scratch." The way she said it made it seem like it was her own personal recipe or something.

"Sounds amazing!" Bryant leaned over and watched me stir some cookies. "You'll save me one, right?" He looked up and winked at me.

Kaitlyn must've missed the memo that Bryant had originally come to see me because she laughed. "Of course. We'll have a plate made up just for you."

"Hey, I can get behind that. Make it a big plate, okay?" He was still looking right at me.

"Okay." I swallowed and then cleared my throat. All of a sudden, I could feel a tightness in my chest. Holy cow. He thought I was going to be at the party. I glanced at my cousins, and neither of them looked too happy. Clarise had already put her foot down, so it wasn't like they'd have to invite me anyway. "I'll give you a whole bunch of goodies on this one," I said as I walked over to the cupboard with the platters. I could feel three sets of eyes on my back as I pulled out a nice big turquoise plate and set it on the counter. "I'll have it right here waiting for you. See? Now you'll know it's yours."

"You rock!" He laughed and then got serious. "Sorry—I can't stay and chat longer or I'd help you out. But my dad texted a few minutes ago. I gotta head home for a bit, but I'll be back for the shindig."

I stayed behind the counter and kept stirring the cookie dough while my cousins walked him to the front door. I needed an excuse to be gone when he came back, except I doubted I'd be able to leave. Clarise would definitely remember that I was grounded if I tried.

The rest of the afternoon was spent preparing snack foods, then dinner for the family, and then more cleaning up. I still hadn't had a chance to shower, or change, or do my hair or makeup, or anything by the time the guests started showing up. I put the finishing touches on the food and pulled the warm things—like taquitos and pizza rolls—out of the oven at the last second, then bolted downstairs.

It was silly, but I didn't want to be the only one in the house who looked like a hot mess. So I changed my clothes and sprayed perfume and slapped on some makeup. My hair was hopeless at this point, so I threw it up in a high ponytail and then went to work cleaning my room. It was nervous energy in excess. I was a complete wreck, but I really didn't have anything else to do. So I straightened up stuff that hadn't been straightened in months and then hung up stuff that hadn't been hung up for months too. I tried to spruce up my creepy little basement storeroom … and then I stopped.

I stared at the white walls and the lack of anything on them. Then I looked at my makeshift bed. It'd been some old queen bed Grandma didn't need anymore. At ten, I was grateful for something big, and didn't understand the significance of not getting to sleep on my own new princess bed Mom had gotten me for my birthday. I could barely remember it—white with high posts and sheer pink and green fabric draped across the top and down the sides. What I really remembered about it was that it was beautiful. And it came with matching white scrolled dressers and a pretty desk. Everything in that room was like walking into a magazine.

Like my cousin's rooms were now. Like the fancy guest bedrooms with their lush mattresses and exotic Indian-fabric pillows.

I blinked and looked again at my old lumpy bed from Grandma's storeroom. It had a plain brown headboard and charming multicolored handstitched quilt for the top. Sure, it wasn't the most stunning bedroom, but it was a space I could use until I found my own.

It hadn't dawned on me until that moment how much of a burden I must be on my aunt and uncle. They had no desire to raise another daughter. Everything in my life since my mom died had been not-so-subtle about pointing to temporary. There was nothing permanent about my living arrangements, or even the way they treated me. I mean, they totally went out of their way and let me have the cat. Of course, I held on to Mrs. Wiggins so hard, I doubt anyone could've pried her out of my hands if they wanted to. And Christmases weren't bad. I was always given nice things. Usually cute clothes and shoes and stuff like that because I'd grown out of the others.

But…

I went into the closet and put on my jacket. Then I slowly made my way upstairs and out the side door. Happy chatter followed me out the door as I shut it. I was grounded, so I knew I couldn't leave the house, but technically, the backyard wasn't leaving, right? It was dark. Even the lights from the windows didn't catch me as I walked all the way to the back of the yard.

Growing up in Flagstaff, Arizona, wasn't too bad. When I say I'm from Arizona, people always assume that means we have hundred-degree weather during the winter. Which isn't true. Sure, down in Phoenix, their Februarys have been known to scorch every now and then, but up here in Flag? Yeah, we get snow. A lot some winters, but it always melted before too long. Tonight was cold, though—a bit colder than normal.

I climbed onto the trampoline and lay down, looking up at the stairs in the chill of the February evening. There were so many stars out there. It was beautiful and vast and lonely.

My mouth turned down as I took a deep breath. "Mom?"

I didn't know what to say. I only knew that I missed her, and I wished more than anything she was there right now so I didn't have to be here.

I could feel my headache returning, so I closed my eyes and imagined being still. I must've dozed off because the next thing I remembered was waking up freezing and Bryant climbing onto the trampoline with me.

"Do you have any idea how hard it is to find someone who doesn't want to be found?" he said as he scooted next to me. "Are you cold? You've got to be. How long have you been out here?" He wrapped his arms around me and tucked me face-forward up against him.

Instant warmth flooded my body from head to toe. It felt so good to be held.

"I wasn't hiding," I murmured into his jacket.

"Ha. You were *so* hiding. I don't believe that for a second." He squeezed me in closer. "And I know you were hiding from me, so don't even start."

"I wasn't—I promise. Did you get your plate of goodies?"

"They were awesome, but it was missing something."

"What?"

"You."

"Sorry."

"Are you shy? Is that it? Do you hate being around a ton of people?" he asked quietly.

I thought of the large birthday parties and events my mom would always take me to.

"Not really. I don't like to be reminded of hard things, but I'm not shy."

"So am I hard to be around, then?"

I grinned. "No. Yes, well, a little. Bryant, I wasn't hiding from you."

"Then why didn't you come watch movies with us?"

Because if I did, I wouldn't hear the end of it for years, and I'm not the disobedient type. Because I wasn't invited, and no one wants to be the odd man out. Because they were probably lame movies, and who wants to waste their time watching lame movies? Because I'm a cousin, not a friend. Because no one wanted me there. Because I've never been included for a movie night in all the years I've lived here, and if I showed up today, it would be… "It was a long day. I was tired."

"So instead, you cleaned your bedroom and then went outside and fell asleep in the cold on a trampoline?"

I guessed he went searching for me in my room first. "Something like that."

"Indy?"

"Yeah?"

"When your aunt called you upstairs earlier, what did she want?"

My heart turned to brick. "Um, she needed me to do some jobs that I hadn't got done."

I felt his warm breath cascade over my hair and down my cheeks. "So, she knew you had company, told Jayda and Kaitlyn I was downstairs with you, waited until they went down, and then called you up?"

I took a few deep breaths, trying to get this ridiculous imaginary weight off my chest. "Something like that."

"And then made you do chores?"

I shrugged.

"Did part of your jobs include preparing food for your cousin's party tonight?"

"Yes."

I felt a small kiss being placed on the top of my head. It was oddly comforting. "And did you hide away from me because you knew I was coming?"

My voice came out as barely a whisper. "No."

I heard him inhale and then slowly blow his breath out. "Then is the reason why you didn't come to the party was because you weren't invited?"

I didn't say anything. My throat closed up, and I couldn't say a word even if I wanted to.

After a few seconds, he tried again. "Were you told not to come?"

I honestly became solid. There was no way I was going to answer that question either.

"Indy?"

I closed my eyes. "Yes?"

"After I checked downstairs for you, I had a hunch you might be out back. I don't know how I knew, only that I could tell you hadn't gone far. But I didn't expect to find you so cold, or so lonely. And after putting together everything you've said and how you're acted—all of it—I've come to realize that you've needed a friend like me for a very long time. Can you forgive me for being caught up in my own mess and not seeing you until now?

"Bryant, what you are talking about? I'm fine."

"Shh … No, you're not. Not really. You're barely here. You're only hanging on because you have to."

"Whatever."

"Now the question left is—what am I going to do with my little Cinderella?"

Chapter 8

"I'm not your Cinderella," I grumbled. "Cinderella is long gone. She was a silly game my mom and I played—and yes, my mother was obsessed with Cinderella, hence my first and middle names." And could I possibly say the word "Cinderella" more in one breath?

Bryant chuckled and kissed the top of my head again. "It is the most perfect name for you."

I half pretended to push against him. "I think I'm going to be sick. It is *not* a perfect name for me. It's a hideous name. I prefer Indy much better."

"Yes, I know, but it's fun to tease you. I have a feeling you don't get teased enough. Thank goodness I've started coming around. Could you imagine how boring your life would be without me?"

No. Now that he was here, I couldn't imagine not having him, and that sort of completely terrified me. "Okay, let's slow down a little. I don't even know you—you don't even know me."

"Actually, I know you more than you think. That's what this is—we're getting to know each other. It's how all relationships start."

I didn't think my heart could take another second of anything today. It was seriously at its limit. "So . . . *are* we starting a relationship here?"

"I don't know. Are we? Besides, all friendships are relationships."

I clutched his jacket and held on for a minute, just to quiet my buzzing nerves and the thoughts jumbling in my head. "This is going to be very complicated. I don't think you realize how much."

"Why? The only thing complicating anything right now is fear." He sighed. "Look, Indy. I like you. I want to get to know more about you. Everything you say only makes me more intrigued."

"I don't really have a family."

"And?"

I tried to explain better. "I'm just here because they had to take me in. Now, I don't think my aunt and uncle realize I feel this way. I'm sure they think they're awesome parents to me. And they are—ish. But I don't have someone to talk to and learn from. They're not the type."

"Okay."

Now the hard part. "And they're very protective of me."

"Meaning?" Bryant asked.

"Meaning, I don't get to do a lot of things. Technically, if they knew I was out here on the trampoline with you, they'd—"

"Lose it?"

"Yeah, understatement there. I'm grounded right now. Actually, I'm always grounded. I mean, it happens so frequently, I think it's more of a way to keep me safe or something."

"Are your cousins grounded a lot too?"

I pulled back to try to find his eyes in the dark. I could make out shadows—I knew where they were—but I couldn't see them. "No."

"So your aunt and uncle ground you constantly?"

"Pretty much."

"Which means they'd ground you from having a boyfriend, or a boy who's a friend."

"Oh, definitely. I don't even have to ask."

"But your cousins have relationships?"

"Yep."

"That's messed up."

"Or . . ." I attempted to give some sort of alternative here. "They don't know what to do with me, or how to take care of me, because I'm just their sister's orphaned daughter. Some people aren't really good with the 'loving someone else's kid' thing. Maybe it's just that."

"It's still messed up." He chuckled softly. "So, what are you saying here?"

"I'm saying you're better off trying for a friendship with one of my cousins than with me."

"But what if I don't want to get to know them better?"

I bit my lip. "Well, from today, I'd say they'd definitely like to get to know you."

"Yes, but . . ." He bent his head and surprised me by kissing my nose. "I have this thing. I like girls who are kind." Then he caused me to giggle when his nose rubbed on my chin. "And as far as I can see, they're not very kind."

"But I was telling you off." I wondered if he was going to try to kiss my lips.

"That doesn't count. You were in survival mode and using self-defense and all that. But then this girl came out—the one who tries to protect her family, even if they're rude to her. So hush and let me hold you." His arms were so secure and strong, and I felt unbelievably safe. I sighed and could feel the start of tiny little butterflies zooming from my neck all the way down my spine. Honestly, if he'd told me to run away with him right then and there, I might've seriously considered it.

Later when I pulled back, he kissed my forehead and then my nose again. I couldn't stop giggling. And I couldn't remember a time when I felt so pretty and crazy happy. "You're too good for me," I said.

"I could stay here on this freezing trampoline and hear you laugh all night long. There's something awesome about hearing a girl laugh after she's hated you."

"Is that why you're here? You don't want me to hate you?"

"No. I'm here because you mean that much to me, and I still haven't figured out why yet."

"So, once you figure it out, you'll take off again?" I asked worriedly.

"Indy! Stop." He pulled back.

"Sorry. Apparently, I have abandonment issues."

"And ten hours ago you wanted to kick me out of the house."

I winced. "Don't remind me." I waited a few moments and then asked, "Okay. So if we do get together, then what?"

I could feel him shrug. "We see where this goes. And if it works out, great. If it doesn't work out, that's okay too."

A small sliver of panic began to take over. "I don't know. I just can't see it working." Before he could answer, I said, "Hear me out. You and I are from completely different worlds. Sure, this feels good right now, like we've connected on a higher level. But we have different friends, different likes and dislikes. And even if you're brave enough to say that everything will be fine at school, it won't be."

"So, what are you trying to say?"

How could I put this without hurting him? "You're not really the type of person I hang out with."

"Meaning?"

"Good grief. You're going to kill me here!"

"Hey, if you're going to make rash statements about how we're not good for each other, you'd better believe I'm going to force you into telling me everything."

I bunched up part of his jacket in my fist. "You're Bryant Bailey, for crying out loud. This isn't that difficult to understand. I've seen you walk around at school—girls practically fall at your feet. Look at my cousins! That's exactly what happens to you everywhere you go. And I'm . . . well, I'm not that way. I don't *want* to be that way. I've worked dang hard to be ignored by your friends, and I'd prefer to keep it like that."

"Indy Zimmerman, you are one tough cookie to figure out."

"Cookie? Cookie? Really, that's the best you could come up with?" I mock-pushed against him.

"Fine. *Girl.* But girl sounds boring." He suddenly wrapped his arms around me and pulled me in close again. "Look. How about we try it your way. I'm not about to lose you, and I think I know what you're trying to say, so I'll respect that."

I was so confused. "What's my way? The *no* relationship part?" My heart felt a little panicked.

"No. You forgot the 'I'm not about to lose you' part. I'm not. So what if we did this under the radar? Sort of relaxed and chill and something no one knew about. Just become close friends and see what happens. Would you like to try that for a couple of weeks and see how it goes?"

"Be secret friends?"

"Yeah. Then your cousins won't get jealous, and your aunt and uncle won't freak out."

"But isn't that dishonest?"

"I don't see why. We're not going to deny it if anyone asks, but we're just not going to flaunt it, either. We'll sort of ease into it this friendship slowly."

For some reason, I was okay with this. "Kind of a trial-and-error type thing. If it doesn't work out, it won't be huge drama all over the school? And without the stress of an actual relationship?"

"Right."

"I like the idea of going slow." I grinned, but it was completely wasted on him in the dark.

"Okay. So how will we keep in touch? Do you have a phone?"

"Yeah, somewhere. I'll have to find it. It's just a text-slash-talk phone. Not an iPhone or anything."

"Hey, that's perfect. Let's plan on talking some nights, if you can, and texting during the day."

"Okay." I was beginning to have hope. At the very least, it could be really fun.

"I'll text you my email address—oh! We can hook up on Facebook, too."

"Whoa. I don't know about Facebook. Everyone will see."

He kissed my forehead again. "You're exasperating. You know that?"

If only he'd get up the nerve and actually kiss me, maybe I won't feel so weird about having kissed him earlier. Gah. "Clearly, you have no idea how irritating you are. So I guess that makes us even!"

He laughed and began to roll off the trampoline. "Come on, Cinderella. Let's get you back in the house before you turn into a pumpkin."

"More like a frozen pumpkin," I grumbled as I followed him. Without his warmth, I could feel the breeze slice through my coat. "And don't call me Cinderella."

He helped me down. "Too late. It's going to happen. Besides, I don't know if you've noticed, but your aunt and cousins are pretty much playing their parts down to a T."

"Whatever. You're such a dork." I didn't protest when his large hand enveloped mine.

"Yes, but I'm your dork now."

I couldn't help it. I smiled a huge, ridiculous smile. "I think I like the sound of that."

"Good, because I believe it'll be the start of amazing things."

I really hoped he was right.

Chapter 9

Sunday morning started out typically. I had been up for a few hours the night before, cleaning up the party mess. Now I was doing my typical Sunday chores. Scrub the tubs, change the sheets, and straighten the cupboards. It was nice, because that's when everybody left to do their shopping, so I had the whole place to myself.

I didn't have an iPod, but I usually turned on some music and jammed while I worked. This time, however, I couldn't help imagining a certain tall, dark-haired, annoying guy dancing with me. He was completely distracting and made me blush, but the daydream made me feel girly and laugh at myself.

"Indy! What is all this? You haven't even loaded the dishwasher yet? And why is this music on?" Clarise asked as she came into the living room earlier than usual.

"Sorry!" I ran and stopped the music coming from the family laptop on the table, and then began to load the dishwasher. "I'll put the laptop back in a minute."

Jayda and Kaitlyn walked into the house with some bags.

Clarise looked around the kitchen and then shook her head. "You'd better."

Jayda walked up to the sink and dropped the water bottle she'd taken with her to the mall into it. "You forgot this."

"Thanks," I muttered as I took off the lid and set it in the dishwasher next to me. What would they do without me there to do such hard chores for them?

As Clarise walked out of the kitchen, she called over her shoulder, "You're grounded for using that laptop."

Nice. That was the one I used for my homework. Now what?

***

On Monday in school, during English, I received my first text from Bryant.

Hey. I miss you.

Four little words, and I didn't think it was possible to feel this giddy. Holy cow, my whole body zinged with warmth. I tried to control my smile as I glanced around the room. I was pretty sure no one noticed me using my notebook to hide my phone, but the way I'd completely forgotten I was in a classroom full of students for a minute scared me.

I decided not to answer him back right away. I was afraid he wouldn't stop, and I'd for sure get caught. I bit my lip as I placed the phone upside down and imagined a world where this became the norm.

Mr. Parkington droned on. "As we explore the findings in Shakespeare's *Hamlet*, I want you to pay particular attention to page…"

I could barely hang on. Four words, and they completely made my day. I didn't think school would ever end. I felt like squealing inside like a little kid, but I didn't. I held myself together—ish.

When the bell rang, I bolted out of English class so fast, I was the first one out. I didn't know Bryant's schedule, but now everything was on override as I searched for him. I knew we'd passed each other in the halls a lot. I knew he'd managed to show up randomly in some of my classes, but for the life of me, I couldn't remember which class or when, or anything.

Why didn't I pay attention the last two weeks when Bryant went overboard with the begging forgiveness thing?

"Indy!"

I whirled around in the busy hallway to find Maxton heading toward me. "Where'd you go? I was waiting for you outside Mr. Parkington's room like usual, but you'd already left."

Oh, dang. I forgot that Maxton and I went to lunch together. How could I have forgotten? What was wrong with me?

"Sorry. I got out early and thought I saw someone." I tried to paste a smile on my face as I walked to my locker, but I already had this huge grin, so it didn't matter.

"What's gotten into you?" He chuckled. "You look like you're walking on air."

"The expression is 'sunshine.'" I bit my lip again. "I'm walking on sunshine."

His eyebrows rose. "Right. So, anything new?"

"Not really," I lied as we approached my locker. I whizzed through my combination and opened it up. We stuffed it full with Maxton's books and backpack, as well as my own, and I slammed it closed. Then I remembered my phone was still in my bag. "Uh, hang on! I forgot something." It took another minute or so, but I finally slipped my phone into my pocket and smiled. "Okay. You hungry?"

He gave my pocket a funny look, but thankfully, he didn't say anything about it. "Sure." Maxton was one of the cool guys who didn't invade too much. It's why we got along so well. He was smart and fun, and pretty much as easygoing as you could get. We'd been hanging out for about three years now. Not too bad, for me and my need to "hide," as Bryant would call it.

Maxton came from a family with a ton of kids, and the last year or so, his dad had been laid off, finding it hard to get another job that would give his family benefits. Even though we had an open campus and you could pretty much drive anywhere to lunch, we chose to stay in the cafeteria. Maxton was on the free lunch program, and that meant cafeteria food.

I was on the "he's pretty much my best friend" program, so I stayed with him.

By the time we'd sat down at the table with our food, Maxton must've decided he was curious about me—or maybe I was acting more different than I thought—because he said, "All right. Spill. What's going on?"

I took a bite of my chicken sandwich and shrugged. "Nothing much."

"Anything new with your aunt and uncle? Jayda? Kaitlyn?"

"Not that I know of."

Maxton looked at me for a moment and then pushed his tray away. "Come on—I'm not stupid. I'm your friend, remember? Now share, or I'm going to get a complex already."

"What? When have you ever had a complex about anything?"

"You're avoiding the question." He pulled his tray back. "All right, I get it. You don't want to tell me anything. Fine. But just know that I know something happened, and the next time you decide you want to hear some of my news, I'll leave you hanging too."

"Not fair." I laughed. Maxton usually had some very juicy gossip.

He finished off his sandwich and then put his elbows on the table. "So, are you going to tell me or not?"

"It's a secret." I totally started to blush. I couldn't believe it. "I don't think I'm supposed to tell anyone."

"I'm not just anyone. Holy cow, I don't think I've ever seen you this red before." He turned more fully toward me. "That's it. Tell me now. Hurry. There's no one else around."

It was true. Only about forty people stayed on campus to eat—most opted to go home or get fast food if they had the money. Maxton and I always had our own table, the one in back where we could eat in peace.

"Fine." I huffed as I leaned over. "But you can't tell anyone."

"Who would I tell?" He looked shocked.

"I mean it." I pointed at him. "You might want to, but you've gotta keep your mouth shut. Or I'll get busted."

His eyes were huge. "What in the . . .? What did you do?"

"Oh, good grief! Nothing bad. Sheesh. Thanks. It's good to know your first thought is that I've done something illegal."

"Well, you said you'd get busted."

He had a point, but I refused to acknowledge it. "Whatever. No, the secret is that Bryant Bailey and I have decided to get to know each other better."

"What?"

"Ish."

"What?"

"Not really, just . . . well, yeah, we are. We're keeping it on the down low, though, because of a lot of complications, but yes. I mean, we talked about it and snuggled on the trampoline out back and everything."

"Wait. What?"

"Are you just going to sit there and say 'what'?"

"What?" He grinned. "No. But seriously, are you kidding?"

"No." I took a deep breath and grinned this silly love-struck grin—at least, I assumed it was a love-struck grin—and shook my head. "He came over Saturday and surprised me and finally talked some sense into me and shared his awful past, and it seems like we have a lot in common."

"Bryant Bailey? *The* Bryant Bailey?"

"Yes."

"The guy you completely despise, who killed your cat and has been stalking you this whole month to apologize for destroying your life—*that* Bryant Bailey?"

"Yes."

"Wow." Maxton leaned back in his chair and flipped his hair out of his eyes. "Wow."

"I know. It's crazy, right?"

"I never would've expected it. Ever."

"Me neither." I leaned forward. "Believe me, I tried everything I could to stay mad at him, but he's pretty much irresistible."

"Is he really? And you just let him hold you?"

"Technically, yeah. He's good at cuddling. Also, I sort of kissed him."."

"Wait. What?" His jaw dropped.

"You sound like a broken record." I grinned.

"I feel like a broken record. This is pretty shocking." He rubbed his face and shook his head.

"I know, right?"

"And him following you around and being persistent worked?"

"Yeah, I guess so."

"Why do I have a feeling that if I followed around—say, one of your cousins—and kept pestering them, I'd get arrested?"

I hated to admit it, but he was right. "Well, I don't think they're as nice as I am."

"Probably not." He took a deep breath and then asked, "So, tell me what happened when you brought me up. I mean, he must have seen us together at PE on Friday, and I know he's seen us other days too. Didn't that sort of put a chink in his armor?"

I was a little lost. "What do you mean?"

He still looked at me in shock. "I mean, what did he say when you told him you already had a boyfriend?"

Chapter 10

I felt my whole body slowly turn to stone. I'm sure my mouth dropped open as well, but I was too numb to notice. Did Maxton really think we were going out? How was this possible? The guy had never once asked me on a regular date, or kissed me, or anything. After a few stunned seconds, I knew I couldn't be completely frozen because I could feel my stomach churning.

I was sick. This type of thing never happened to me. I thought I'd made it clear eons ago that I didn't want boyfriends or relationship junk, that I just wanted friends. And Maxton was cool with that. At least, he said he was.

"Maxton?"

"Yeah?"

I didn't even know what to say. I definitely didn't want to hurt the guy—I mean, he was my closest friend, but I had no idea he had any feelings for me at all. I thought back over the years and the time we'd spent working on assignments, or argued about political stuff, or a couple of times when we played video games in the den. I asked the only thing I could think of. "When did you start liking me?"

"Indy, I've always liked you. From the very beginning, I told you I had a crush on you."

"And what did I say?"

"That you didn't want a boyfriend, so I hung back and we were just friends. Until last year."

My eyebrows shot up. "Last year?"

The bell rang, and it was like I came awake. Suddenly, I realized I was still sitting in the cafeteria, talking to Maxton, and I should have been halfway across the school by now. Dr. Applewood did not take kindly to anyone being late to biology.

We dumped our trays and headed to my locker. I handed over Maxton's things, and then grabbed mine. Then we sort of stared at each other for a minute. "We'll talk later," I said, hoping to regain some sort of normalcy.

"Okay."

I backed up to shut the locker and head to class just as Maxton moved forward, so I accidentally pushed the door into him. "Sorry."

He laughed. "No worries."

What was he doing?

I moved him out of the way and shut the door right as Maxton leaned in and kissed me. Gah! It was by far the most surprising thing that had ever happened to me at school. And it was totally awkward, but not horrible. Just not expected, I guess.

He pulled back and smiled. "See ya later." I watched as he walked down the opposite way I was going. When did his shoulders get so broad?

I closed the locker and then slumped into it. I was completely clueless about what to do next. I'd never expected one guy to kiss me, let alone two.

My phone vibrated, and I pulled it out to see another text from Bryant.

Still miss you. I think I need to do something to fix this.

My heart leaped into my throat, and a huge smile made its way across my face. And I might have giggled. All right, I admit it. I totally did. But then I remembered Maxton, and suddenly everything seemed much more confusing than it was supposed to be.

The warning bell rang, and everyone cleared out of the hall. Then out of the blue, Bryant turned the corner, and he stopped.

He laughed, and then covered his mouth and gestured for me to come to him. I had to head that way anyway, so I did. "What are you doing here?" he asked.

"I was gonna ask you the same thing."

"I thought you were supposed to be in the science wing."

"I am."

His gaze swept over my features. "Did you get my texts?"

I sighed and bit my lip. My stupid smile would not leave my face. Everything about him was so much more exciting than I could ever have imagined.

He looked up and down the nearly deserted hall and pulled me into a small alcove by the drinking fountains. Then he leaned down and hugged me really tight. "That's better. Now one more for the road." He hugged me again. "Bye," he whispered and then swiftly walked out of the alcove and toward his class as if nothing had happened.

"Bye!" Grinning like an idiot, I stepped out and then booked it down the hallway. I was going to be late. Totally late, but in the rules of lateness, this had to be worth it. Bryant Bailey was totally adorkable, and I loved it.

It wasn't until my last class, Algebra II, that I had a chance to text Bryant back. After the test, we had about twenty minutes of free time to chill and talk, or whatever. I stared at the phone at least ten minutes before I had the guts enough to text something. It had to be fun, but not crazy, and kinda flirty too. My anxiety levels went haywire as I pushed send.

I like your way of fixing things.

I swear not even ten seconds later, he replied.

Do you? I miss you again. We should probably fix that.

I tried not to chuckle out loud. It was hard. After a minute or so, I answered back.

When? Where?

My, aren't we eager? Methinks the lady doth loveth my presence.

. . .

What is this ". . ."? Are you blushing too much to answer properly?

I rolled my eyes. *No.*

Liar.

I blushed even redder. *It's not nice to tease girls.*

I know, but it sure is fun. Meet you at the park near your house.

Uh, when?

After school? I don't know. How about 3:45?

I thought of all the chores I had to do and the odds of actually being able to leave the house once I got home. *There's no way. I can't. :(*

Hmm… How do you get to school? Walk? Bus?

I could probably leave early tomorrow morning and not ride in with Kaitlyn and Jayda. *Maybe walk.*

Okay. What if I walked you to school?

I thought he lived about two blocks behind us, and school was about half a mile or so down the road. *Would we take the back roads?*

Of course.

Then all at once, I had a better idea. *What are you doing right now?*

Waiting for the bell to ring. You?

Yeah.

Can we meet now? Are you walking home?

No. I have my car. Want a ride?

Too obvious. Besides, we've got a problem. Well, I do.

What's that?

The bell rang, and I scrambled to finish the text. *Maxton thinks I'm his girlfriend.* I quickly stuffed my backpack and headed out the door—right into Bryant.

"Are you his girlfriend?" he asked casually, walking next to me.

I looked straight ahead. "No. At least, when he asked me a couple of years ago, I told him no. But now he thinks we are. And I don't even know why."

"Have you guys kissed?"

"No. Well, yeah. Today."

"Wait. What?" Bryant stopped in the middle of the busy hallway and then brought us into an empty room and shut the door. "When did he kiss you?"

"After I told him about us getting to know each other more."

Bryant looked shocked. "What? You told him? After you said we couldn't tell anyone and had to be secretive and all that?"

I laughed. I couldn't help it—he looked so funny. "He's my best friend. He could totally tell something was up by the way I was acting. So after he hounded me, I finally shared my news, since I figured he deserved to know more than anyone—except it backfired on me."

"What'd he say?'

"He wanted to know if I'd told you I already had a boyfriend."

"And?"

"Well, I froze. I wasn't expecting that, and I didn't want to hurt his feelings and everything was just weird. Then the bell rang. And I guess because I told him I kissed you this weekend, he felt the need to kiss me. So he did. In the hallway, by my locker."

"You let him kiss you in front of everyone?"

"I didn't know it was going to happen. I told him we'd talk later, and I don't know—I feel like everything in my life has flipped one-eighty, and I don't know what to do."

He was quiet for a bit and then said, "Well, I think you know exactly what you should do."

I looked up at him. All of a sudden, he was a whole lot closer to me. "What?"

"I think you should take a minute and think about which one of us you want more."

"What do you mean?" My rear end bumped into the door, and Bryant rested his arm above my head. I could smell his cologne, and it was making me forget pretty much everything else.

"Well, in my opinion, good ol' Max has definitely got a lead on me."

"Why would you say that?"

"Because you actually like to talk to him. You've been friends for years." He leaned in closer, and my eyelids fluttered shut from his nearness. Then he whispered, "And he's your type."

My lids flew back open, and I stared at his nose before looking into those dark, smoldering eyes. I hadn't ever been close to him like this—not touching, yet so intense. My whole insides were squealing over the tension between us. His lips were mere centimeters away from mine. "Why would you say that?"

"Because he loves everything you do."

"How would you know? You don't even know everything I do."

I gasped as Bryant's lips moved up and skimmed my nose. He was really good at soft kisses. "I don't, but I bet he does."

"Ugh." I growled under my breath. "Why are we discussing Maxton right now?" Good grief—what did I have to do to get the guy to actually kiss me?

He chuckled quietly and kissed my forehead. "Because I like torturing you."

"You're very good at it," I grumbled.

Pulling back, he looked into my eyes again, and I swear I melted. Right then and there. "When you're deciding between us, I want to give you something to remember me by."

"What?" I winced. "You're not serious, are you? You really want me to decide? What if I've already made my decision?"

"Nope." Bryant kissed my nose again. "Then you haven't given Maxton a chance. And I want you to."

If I wasn't completely melted into goo, with only the door propping me up, I'd have seriously considered decking him. "What kind of twisted, melodramatic nonsense is this? Maxton and I have been friends for years. That's it. Just friends."

Bryant silenced my rant with a slow kiss on the cheek. I took a ragged breath. Who knew being kissed on the cheek could feel like that? But when he pulled back, he still insisted on this stupid Maxton thing. "I'm serious, Indy. I think it'd be good for you." His dark eyes found mine again, and I could hardly breathe. "I'm amazed at this attraction I have for you. It's all I can think about."

Eeeh! He felt it too. I grinned. Until his next words.

"But it probably isn't healthy for either of us right now."

"What—why?" I barely recognized my whiny voice.

"Because this is coming on too strong, too fast." He took a deep breath. "If we're meant to have something here, nothing will stop it. But I can't . . . you shouldn't . . . we're not ready for this."

Of all the nerve. After begging me to give us a chance, and now this? He thinks we're going too fast?

"Okay, wait. I can see you're getting mad. Let me finish. I know relationships. I know how this works. When it comes too fast, it leaves just as quickly. Indy, I have a feeling you're going to mean more to me than something fleeting and quick. And you . . . you've only begun to heal from your past. You've got to get to know yourself. So I suggest that we take a step back. Let Maxton in. Let him show you what it's like to date someone your type. And then, once you decide for yourself which guy you'd really rather be with, I'll be here. Waiting for you."

I couldn't help it. His annoying suggestion was making me snarky. "And what if it isn't you? What if this decision to walk away before anything's begun hurts so much that I'm not willing to risk it again? What then, Mr. Confident Bailey, positive that when I'm ready, I'll come running back to you? What then?"

He grinned, a slow, smug grin. "Oh, you'll be back. I'll make sure I'm not too far away. Don't worry." And then he gave me a long bear hug. . All perfect and wonderful and melty. "And that's to make sure you won't forget me, either."

"I hate you," I said against his wonderfully cologned chest.

"I know." He laughed and pulled away, that gorgeous gaze locking with mine again. "Trust me, okay? I care too much about us right now. So go, learn—find you. Find out about life—grow. I'll be here. I'll be the friend you can vent to. I'll be your Maxton."

• • •

I rolled my eyes to break away from his. "You're so full of it. I already have a Maxton! Why do I need another one?"

He shook his head. "Oh, no. Maxton is long gone—you'll see. He'll never be the same again now."

Chapter 11

All at once, I felt the heavy weight of the world settle on my shoulders. "Oh. I hadn't thought of that." Bryant was right. I knew he was right. I'd just lost my best friend. I moved forward, wrapped my arms around Bryant's waist again, and squeezed tight. "Don't leave me. I'll need a friend more than a boyfriend or anything else."

"You don't have anyone to turn to, I know. And I'm sorry." He rubbed my back. "I promise, I'm not going anywhere. And I won't complicate things more than they are. Let's find Indy. Then later, we'll have time for all this crazy talk."

I took a deep breath and thanked whatever weird part of fate that had sent me this guy. "Fine. Though I'm still not promising anything about Maxton."

"You will. You'll like him. And it'll be good for you."

"Will you stop with all this good-for-me junk?"

"Nope. Not going to stop."

"Bryant?"

"Yes?"

"Why did Maxton have to go and ruin everything? Why couldn't he be happy with being my friend and get excited when I finally began to think of building something new?"

Bryant laughed. "Do you honestly think that guy wasn't in love with you? He didn't ruin anything—he only opened the playing field for you."

"Life isn't some game! I don't want to play on a field. I want things easy."

"No. You want to hide, but you can't anymore. You need to experience life and move and grow."

I banged my forehead against his chest, but at the same time, I felt kind of relieved too. He was guaranteeing me a way to have his steadiness in my life—which was what I craved most—without the odd relationship stuff. Maxton, I could deal with. This new super-hot Bryant was a little harder to work out. If I was completely honest with myself, I really only wanted him as a best friend anyway. Well, maybe a best friend I could kiss.

He pulled away and started to open the door behind me. "Come on. Let's get you out of here before Maxton starts tearing the place down, looking for you."

"Whatever. He won't even notice I'm gone."

Bryant's eyebrows shot up. "You're in denial now. Any guy would be searching for you. Trust me on this."

"I wouldn't trust you farther than I could throw you."

He pushed me out into the hall. "I'd like to see you try to pick me up, let alone throw me."

"I've done it plenty of times in my dreams. Just chucked you into the nearest river."

"Oh! So now you admit that you dream about me?"

"I was not—well, not in that way." I'd have to learn not to take his bait. We began to walk down the hall, and I knew I was going to have to face Maxton soon. "What do I say?"

Bryant didn't even ask what I was talking about. "You tell him that you and I had a talk, and you told me that you and he already had a past together."

"I am not saying that!" I hissed.

"Fine. Then tell him I'm making you decide which guy is better."

I shoved against his arm. "You're not helping."

"What?" He laughed. "I'm giving you ideas here. Can't you be a little bit grateful?"

"I'll be grateful when I get away from you."

"Aha! There she is. There's my Indy. Gotta love your charm."

I grinned and turned to chew him out, but—

"Indy! There you are." Maxton came up to me and wouldn't even look at Bryant. Which I'm sure made Bryant chuckle. "Where have you been? Do you need a ride?"

Boy, he wasn't wasting any time staking his claim. I watched Bryant to gauge his reaction, and he nodded for me to accept the offer. I was thankful he didn't actually push me at Maxton. I took a second to study the big dork, and then, while still staring into Bryant's eyes, I nodded. It was time to find out who I was, and Maxton deserved a chance to get to know me. The real me. He'd gone out of his way for me the last few years, and it wouldn't kill me to see where this goes. Besides . . . I grinned. His kiss wasn't that bad. "Yeah, I'd love a ride. Thanks for asking."

I turned on my heel and didn't look back as I headed down the hall with Maxton.

As I climbed into Maxton's car, I could feel my phone vibrate. I pulled it out and grinned. Bryant.

I'll call tonight.

***

Maxton wasn't too weird on the drive home. I mean, there was definitely a new awkward tension between us, but it didn't have to be considered bad. He was a lot more confident than I thought he'd be—almost excited, even.

"So, how was school?" he asked.

"Interesting." I grinned. "Full of all sorts of new ideas and revealing stuff."

"How so?"

"I don't know. Just was." I looked out the window and then asked the question that had been bugging me since lunch. "What happened last year that changed us?"

"Are you talking about how I knew you had a thing for me?"

I closed my eyes and didn't know whether to blush or wince because something had happened and I still had no clue what it was. "Sure."

"Don't you remember last summer?" He glanced over. When I didn't say anything, he continued. "You were sick and asked me to come over. So I snuck out of my house and stayed in your room and chatted with you all night so you'd feel better. Then I had to get out before your family woke up."

What? He thought that was the moment when I proved I was in love with him? I was half delirious and definitely not thinking. If I'd been thinking, I never would've begged him to come over so late at night.

"Yeah? I remember. You were really great that night."

He rubbed his lips together and focused on the road. "The thing is, that night I really saw how fun you were. Sure, you were totally loopy and crazy sick, but you were still nice. And for the first time, you showed me how scared you were. It was interesting, seeing this tough girl being so vulnerable and actually needing someone. That night didn't just teach me how much you needed me—it taught me how much I needed you. We bonded." He looked at me. "You can't deny it."

"I—I don't. You're right. We did." I took a deep breath and looked out the window at my side. "I'm sorry if I hurt you with Bryant today. I didn't mean to." My head whirled around with so many thoughts, but mostly, that memory in July came hurtling back. Maxton was right—I'd been scared and alone and so very needy. My fever had gotten too high, and I couldn't sleep and I wanted a friend. I wanted someone to care about me.

My aunt and uncle weren't the type who liked to be woken up when you were sick. And they definitely didn't like to know when you threw up, or any of that kind of stuff. They really didn't do "sick" at all, as evidenced by how Clarise had let me sleep in Saturday and actually made Kaitlyn and Jayda help her clean. So back in July, I was miserable and called the person I could depend upon most.

So, that was what love was? Not make-out sessions and hot dates and long letters or ridiculous poetry and flowers and all that. It was a guy who took the chance of getting in trouble to spend time with the girl who asked him to. All in all, I wasn't too excited that Maxton had risked his parents' wrath for me and my breakdown. I definitely wasn't worth it. But it showed a bit more about his character than I'd seen before. This guy fell for me, was in my room all night long, but remained a gentleman. He didn't try to maul me or make out or anything. He respected my boundaries. I got all girly for a minute thinking of how awesome that was—until I remembered that I'd been sick. Yeah, that. He wouldn't have wanted to touch me with a ten-foot pole.

Maxton said, "You didn't hurt me. Don't worry about it."

"What?" I was completely lost.

He looked at me like I was crazy. "Today. At lunch? Remember? Don't worry about an apology. I'm okay. I mean, I was shocked—but you didn't hurt me."

Oh! Yeah. Today. Bryant. I cleared my throat, trying to sound more normal. "So after last summer, why didn't you try to kiss me or something? Why didn't you let me know?"

"Kiss you?" He laughed. "You're not the kissing type. I mean, you weren't then. Now, that's different." He grinned and then looked away.

"What do you mean, it's different?" I tried not to laugh, but really, he was bizarre sometimes.

"I mean, today, after I found out you were willing to begin kissing people, I decided I wasn't going to hold back anymore."

"Oh, well, I noticed that part."

"Did you?"

I rolled my eyes and looked back out the window. "Dork."

"Hey! Don't call me a dork. I'm awesome—admit it!"

"Whatever. You're such a dork, my mom would've called you a doofus!"

"Doofus?" He chuckled. "What in the world is a doofus?"

I couldn't help but smile. "It's bad. It's really bad. It's worse than a dork."

"Great. Now she's calling me vintage names."

"Vintage names?" He really *was* a doofus. I grinned and shook my head as I watched the neighbors' houses as we drove by. I waited a few seconds and then asked, "Why me?"

He pulled into my driveway and put the car into park. "What do you mean? Are you asking why I like you?"

"I guess. Sounds like I'm fishing for compliments, doesn't it? I don't mean to be—wait. Yes, I do. I don't know who I am, and I'm trying to figure it out. So any little help here—anything you see that makes me unique or special, would you let me know?"

"Right." He took another deep breath and then put the car in reverse and looked over his shoulder as he backed out of the driveway.

"Hey! Where are we going?"

"To talk."

"Yeah, but Clarise is going to have a cow."

One eyebrow rose. "Clarise always has a cow. She'll have to get over it today."

"What?" I didn't know whether to laugh or cry. "Maxton, you're killing me!"

"I know, but it's good for you." He gave a smug grin as he headed toward the stop sign down the road.

"Kidnapping me is good for me?"

He slammed on the brakes. Thankfully, he wasn't going that fast, but I still jerked forward. "Seriously? You feel like this is kidnapping?" Pulling over, he looked at me. "Do you not want to talk?"

"Um, I want to talk without getting in trouble."

"Too late. That's going to happen anyway. And you and I both know Clarise wouldn't be happy if I came over." He rubbed his hands through his brown hair, messing it up. "Okay, so I know this has been an odd day for you, but why all the drama? What do you need from me?"

My heart clenched as I looked at this guy for the first time. Really looked at him. His hazel eyes flashed with something I wasn't sure I could identify. Impatience? Pain? Hope? I didn't know. I don't think I'd ever really looked into his eyes before. Maxton's nose was straight, his lips full, and his jaw—when did his jaw get that little bit of stubble? It made him look . . . older. It was weird. I decided to focus on his eyes again and found long eyelashes and nice, lighter-brown eyebrows. Wow. When did Maxton get so hot?

Chapter 12

Beyond all of his hotness, I saw a guy who'd stayed with me. I always assumed until that moment that Maxton was a loner, like me. But . . . "You're in wrestling, aren't you?"

He blinked. I guess the change of subject was a little much, but he went with it. "Yes. Er, but you knew that."

"Yeah. I guess I forgot." I frowned. "Don't you have wrestling practice today or something?"

He pulled back. "Are you trying to get rid of me?" When I looked confused, he said, "Okay. Look. We're getting off on the wrong foot. Let's try this again. No, I don't have practice on Mondays. I've never had practices on Mondays. However, I have a match every Saturday for the next five weeks. And then if I make it to finals and state, it'll be another couple more Saturdays. Does that help?"

"Uh—yeah. More than I needed. But it works." Then I shifted in my seat. "So, do you ever hang out with your team?"

He glanced away and then back at me. "What do you mean? Sure, on the bus and stuff."

"No. I mean, like at school—do they ever invite you over to hang with them or to do things?"

"Well, yeah, all the time."

"Like for lunch?"

He shrugged. "I guess. Cameron's mom makes all the guys healthy lunches on Tuesdays and Thursdays to help them maintain their weight. So I get invited to that all the time."

"Why don't you go with them?"

Maxton looked at me funny and then shook his head. "Um, because I'm hanging out with you."

"So, wait. All this time that we've been having lunch together, you've been doing it because you want to, not because you have to?"

"What are you asking, Indy? You're acting really odd. Just spill it."

"I don't know how to say this." I took a deep breath and tried again. "I don't mean to sound weird—I'm just confused. I thought we stayed in the cafeteria because your dad got laid off and you couldn't afford to eat out. But now you tell me you could've actually have awesome food, but you didn't go. Why?"

"Uh, is this a trick question?" He gave me a funny smile and then laughed. "Because it's sounding like one." He leaned forward. "Look, I like you. Most days, I try to convince myself I'm not in love with you too, but that's a total lie, and I know it. Clarise won't give you money to go out to eat, and she refuses to let you make your own lunches and bring them to school because it's 'tacky.' When you got embarrassed about it and was worried about eating in the cafeteria in high school, I had my mom get me meal tickets too because it wasn't that big of deal to me where I ate, and I knew you wouldn't accept some pity-lunch thing. So I made up a story about my dad getting laid off, and—yes—I shouldn't have said that. Mainly because you ask how my dad is doing all the time, and I have to keep lying to keep the truth from coming out, all because of your stupid pride or whatever. And because I can't help it. You're amazing. And I'll gladly make up more junk just to have an hour with you every day."

I didn't even know what to say. I think my jaw hit the floor about halfway through, but I wasn't quite certain. "So . . . wait. Your wrestling friends—do they know you hang out with me?"

"Um, yes, it's pretty obvious. They tease me about my girlfriend all the time. Mostly, they ask why she never comes to my matches. I tell them it's complicated, but I know it's because you couldn't, even if you wanted to—which I doubt. So I've never really invited you."

How were Maxton and I living two completely different realities, and I never knew it before? My heart sort of grew all warm and fuzzy and then became broken at the same time. I really couldn't explain what was happening. Only that it was something huge. All I knew was that I was a lousy friend. And probably the worst girlfriend on the planet. But in my defense, I had no idea I *was* a girlfriend. For the first time, I was beginning to understand Maxton a little more.

"So, every lunch has been like a date, then?"

He sheepishly looked down. "Maybe. I guess so." Then his smiling eyes met mine again. "I don't know. Look, I'm completely—inexperienced here. I fail at this whole relationship thing. Clearly. Since you're acting like you didn't even know I had a thing for you. So somehow, somewhere, my communication skills bite. But . . . I don't know. I . . . look." I noticed that his hands were twitching.

Wow. He really was nervous. And probably a lot shyer than he let on.

Maxton tried again. "Look. I know I'm not Bryant Bailey. And I'm not trying to be him. He's his own brand of whatever." He shook his head. "Great. I'm rambling. What I'm trying to say is, I like you." His face started to turn red. "Okay, I probably love you, too. And I'd like to start something here. And I'd like a chance before this other guy comes in and sweeps you off your feet. I'd like to at least not be a complete nerd, or doofus, or whatever you want to call me. I'd like to prove to you—" He stopped and cleared his throat. "I like to prove that all this time I've spent with you wasn't just because. I really have put a lot out there, hoping you'd take my hints or return my feelings, or I don't know—care for me too—and I . . . "

He was talking too much. It was becoming ridiculous. Right then, I learned way more about my selfishness than I wanted to admit. All I knew was that Bryant was right. Bryant saw something I never had. He knew—probably the whole school knew—that this completely sweet and wonderful guy had been falling for me all along, and I was clueless to it. As Maxton rambled, I finally did the only thing that made sense. I leaned over and kissed him. Right there on the side of street, in front of one of my neighbors' houses, I kissed Maxton Hoyster. And it was about time.

This kiss was pretty shocking, much better than the simple peck he'd given me in the hallway. In fact, I was surprised to feel the sparks flying. When I moved back, I was pretty sure I wasn't the only one who couldn't catch their breath.

"Um, you kissed me," he said.

"Well, I wanted you to stop talking."

"Huh. Well, it worked." He smiled and put his arm up on the steering wheel. "What was the other reason?"

I decided not to answer that question right away. Instead, I changed the subject. "I want to go to your next wrestling match."

"You mean this Saturday?"

"Yeah. What time does it start? Is it here in Flagstaff?"

He grinned. "Are you kidding me? What will Clarise say?"

Clarise was the last person I wanted to think about right then. Maxton was right—my aunt was always going to be mad. "I'm not going to ask her. I thought if I got caught, I'd beg forgiveness."

He looked shocked. "You're really serious?"

"Well, you've done so much for me, I figured it was time I started to support you. Unless you don't want me there—I completely understand if you don't."

"No! I think it's awesome. I would love to have you cheering me on." Then he got a little sheepish again. "But just so you know, wrestling isn't a pretty sport."

"Pretty?" What in the world was he talking about?

"Yeah, it's not like basketball or soccer where the players run around a lot. This is intense. And we're—well, wrestling each other. Which is, um—guys on top of each other in a battle of concentrated maneuvers to determine who is the stronger of the two players."

I'd never seen a wrestling match, but I'd never thought of it being like what he described.

"Oh, and we wear funny clothes."

"What do you mean?"

"They're like racing swimming suits with attached suspenders."

I had no idea what he was talking about. "Okay."

"Cool." He smiled. "Well, if you're serious, the meet starts at eleven, but the matches for the younger competitors go first, and then I'll be near the end. So if you show up around twelve thirty or so, you should be there in time."

"All right. That sounds like fun."

• • •

He nodded. "Yeah, it'll be exciting having you there to watch me."

"Okay. Sounds like a plan." Suddenly, the conversation sort of stopped, and I wasn't sure what to do. We were still parked outside my neighbor's house, and…

"Indy?"

"Yeah?"

"I know I kind of threw this out there during lunch—mainly because I was jealous of Bryant and couldn't believe I was already losing you before I had a chance—but uh, I was wondering, would you like to be my girlfriend?"

So that was it? That was how guys asked girls? I'd always wondered, and part of me expected it to be flashier, but a huge part of me was glad it wasn't. I definitely didn't love being the center of attention during heartfelt moments. I'd always preferred them to be one-on-one with the person you were with. But I was totally stalling. My eyes searched his as I bit my lip and thought of what Bryant had said. I needed to find me. I need to go with someone who was my type. Maxton was *so* my type.

He was actually cuter than my type, but I wasn't going to hold that against him. I took a deep breath and it caught halfway in my throat, causing me to release a breathy gasp. Bryant and I shared something I was never going to find with anyone else. Especially with our stories being so similar, and he had this way of knowing what I needed and reading into my soul. It was startling. And curious. And wonderful. And terrifying. And powerful. All at the same time.

Maxton was comfortable and easy and fun and sometimes shocking too. But he was steady and loved me, and that was some pretty heady stuff right there. I most definitely knew Maxton would think about me and see me and take care of me. He was pretty much the safest first boyfriend a girl could have. Bryant was right. It was time I found out what it was like to truly live. And that meant learning who I was, and giving Maxton a chance to prove himself.

"You don't have to answer right now," Maxton blurted out, clearly embarrassed by my silence.

"No. It's okay." I smiled. "I was thinking it over—you know me. I'm not the kind of person to leap before I think."

"No, no, you're not." He gave a hopeful grin.

I pushed out all thoughts of jumping into things with Bryant and then simply said, "I would love to be your girlfriend." Then I chuckled and added, "For real now."

Chapter 13

"So, how did the talk with Maxton go?" Bryant's deep voice rumbled through my phone later that night. His voice sent these crazy chills from my ear, down my neck, and tickled the back of my shoulder blade.

I took a shaky breath and answered, "Good."

"Good? That's it? Just good?"

I grinned at his teasing and plopped down on my bed. "Well, what would you like me to say?"

"I don't know, but you gotta actually talk to me." His voice changed a little. "So, do you have a bona fide boyfriend, or not?"

Bona fide? Good grief. I rolled my eyes at his geekiness. "Yes. I have a boyfriend."

"Good for you! Bravo! I knew you could do it!" He sounded a little too excited.

"Well, it's your fault. I hope you remember that when you miss me like crazy the next month or so."

"Month?" I could hear him fake-gasp. "Who said anything about a whole month? I couldn't live that long without you."

"Ha. Ha." I put my arm behind my head and bit my lip to wipe the stupid smile off my face. "So, you were right."

"Wait—what?" I heard something rubbing on the phone. "Hang on. Not sure I heard that correctly."

"Whatever. You heard me."

"Yes, but I want to make sure it's recorded for posterity's sake. This is important. Girls rarely admit when a guy is right, so I need to make this legit. Could you please repeat that?"

I ignored his teasing and got straight to the heart of the matter. "He really does deserve a chance. I didn't know it, but the guy's been turning down good meals to sit with me in the cafeteria all this time because he knows Clarise won't give me any money to go out to eat."

"She doesn't?" He sounded genuinely shocked. "At all? But I see Jayda and Kaitlyn out to eat all the time."

"Well, that's part of their allowance money. If they keep their grades up, they get like forty dollars a week each to eat off campus."

"What have you been doing with your allowance money?"

It's funny how quickly you can go from being all warm and happy and smiley to nearly dropping the phone when your heart turns to lead. I didn't answer.

Bryant growled. "Indy, come on. I'm your new best friend, remember? Now tell me what it's like there."

"Why do you want to know? What I do with my money is my business. Besides, I don't have to tell you all my secrets."

"Yes. Yes, you do."

"Why?"

His voice got quiet and deep again. "Because honestly, I don't think you get an allowance. At all."

How did he know? I sat up and tucked my feet under me. "Why would you say that?"

"What do you do with your allowance money?" He was persistent, wasn't he?

"Are you going to keep hounding me until I tell you?"

"Quite possibly."

"Urgh." I took a deep breath. "Fine. I guess my allowance money goes to pay for my cafeteria lunch."

"Couldn't that be considered child abuse? Forcing a kid to get good grades so they can eat nasty food has to be some sort of offense in Arizona. I'm certain of it."

"Ha. Yeah, no."

He was silent for a minute and then asked, "Do you get any other allowance?"

"No."

"Nothing? Not for shoes, or shampoo, or a random candy bar?"

"What are you talking about? No. But it's no big deal."

"Who buys those things for you?'

"Holy cow, Bryant. My aunt and uncle do. I'm not deprived!"

"Hey, I just have to ask. But I'm glad to hear they take care of the essentials."

I plucked at the blanket under me. "Though, I wish I got my allowance for grades," I said. "I'd make a whole lot more than my cousins do."

"You get good grades?"

"School's pretty easy. And I sort of love learning. Which is great since I have so much time on my hands."

"So what's your allowance for? Cleaning? Chores? Don't your cousins do jobs?"

"They're way too busy. Especially after school. They come home in time for dinner and then they pretty much crash from exhaustion."

"I get what you're saying. Little Cinderella does all the housework and she's grounded a lot, and if she doesn't do everything she's supposed to, Aunt Clarise won't refill her school lunch cards."

He nailed it. I chuckled. "Good grief. When you put it that way, my life sounds horrid."

He didn't say anything. I thought he'd at least laugh or something.

"What?" I asked.

"Indy?"

I couldn't figure out why he wouldn't come out and say it. "Yes?"

"Why are you so nice?"

I laughed. All of this quiet over some false belief that I was nice. "You've gone off the deep end again. Why do you keep coming to the conclusion that I'm nice? Have you forgotten the several death threats I've given you the past few weeks?"

"No, but I deserved those."

"Uh, no one deserves to die over an accident. I was—well, I still am—torked. But I'll get over it."

"Do you miss her?"

"Mrs. Wiggins? Every day." I stopped plucking at the blanket. "I would've been petting her right now. She loved to curl up on my bed with me."

"I wish there was a way I could go back in time and—"

"It's okay, Bryant. If you want to know the truth, she knew better than to go out into that road. She was almost six years old. I don't know why she darted or what she was thinking, but it's actually really bad of me to blame you for something that was no one's fault."

"And now we're back to you being so nice." I could hear him shift around. "I'm serious. You're basically a servant in your own family's home, and you cover for them. And you're sweet when you talk about them. Why is that?"

"Oh, believe me, I think of plenty awful things to say all the time. I don't exactly love cooking and cleaning and being grounded constantly. I guess the real word you're looking for here is 'patient.' Why am I so patient?" I went to pet my cat, but stopped my hand in midair. "I don't know why. Maybe because they're the only real family I have now."

"Well, there is that." He went quiet for a minute and then said, "There's something about you that's addicting, and I think I finally figured it out."

"What?"

"Now hold on and don't interrupt me with obnoxious contradictions. This is what I feel about you—this is how I see you. And remember, you asked for it."

Oh, great. I couldn't even imagine how embarrassing his next words would be.

"You're so addicting because you're an old soul. You see past the negativity—and believe me, you have a lot of negative going on right now—and though you may grumble, you see past it and cope. The hard things thrown your way don't cripple you—you find ways to stay human and caring and leave your footprint on the world."

I clutched the phone tighter to my ear. I'd never considered myself that way, but it was deeply moving.

"Indy, there's this incredibly amazing person under your ultra-snarky and fun personality. I'm not sure why any guy wouldn't want to dig deeper and take the time to get to know you. You have so many layers and hidden secrets in your attempts to shield others from your crazy life—it impresses me. You don't seem the type to sit and gossip about stuff and find things to complain about. I think you're pretty chill with whatever life throws at you."

"I like a little drama and gossip as much as the next girl."

"You do? So you're the type who'll sit and moan to your friends because some other chick wore a pair of shoes you didn't like, or whose makeup wasn't done the way you thought it should be? That's you?"

What in the world? "Er, no. Not now, not ever. I couldn't care less what people wear. If they feel happy and pretty in it, who am I to judge?"

"See? That's what I'm talking about. That's what makes you so—so *mature*, I guess is the word I'm looking for. You're not caught up in petty things, and I can't really see you throwing some massive temper tantrum because you didn't get to use Daddy's car Saturday night."

"The analogy is all wrong, but I understand what you mean."

"So, what's your secret?"

I shrugged and fluffed up my pillow and then slowly scrunched down. "I don't know. I guess when I lost my mom, I realized that there were more important things in life than drama. All of a sudden, I went from being a princess to—well, basically a pauper, and that changed me." I took a deep breath and tried not to think too much about how much I missed her. Instead, I focused on the question and rambled. "I'd always been taught to be kind and caring. Mom was so good about that. To see the other person's perspective. That right there has saved me many nights of being mad at them or causing drama. I don't dwell on what I don't have, but I'm grateful for what I do.

"Anyway, why would I worry about things like what someone wears, or drives, or says, or looks like? Life isn't about trying to conform to someone else's idea of what you should be. Life is about being true to yourself, and kind to all those who aren't quite ready to be true to themselves yet."

"I like that." His voice went deep again. "It makes sense. And it's so right. If people spent less time looking at what to fix in others and more time fixing themselves, we'd have a nearly perfect society."

I laughed. "There's no such thing! And don't expect perfection, either, or you'll never be happy. You've got to allow people to be who they are and accept it as is."

"I'm such a moron."

Where'd that come from? "Why would you say that?"

He grumbled something under his breath and then said, "Because I told you to go for Max, but now I'm missing you too much and want you all to myself."

Chapter 14

I was completely blushing. "Right. On that note, I should probably hang up now."

Bryant chuckled. "Yeah, I guess I deserve that." Then he completely adorably sighed. "But really, what was I thinking? After talking to you now, I realize you probably know you a whole lot better than I know me."

"No. You're right. I don't know who I am. I'm here. I'm living. I'm hanging on day-by-day, but I'm not really growing—you know what I mean? Sure, I know how to be patient-ish with my family and I don't jump into silly first-world problems. But honestly, I don't know what I want. I think college might help me, but I don't even know where to go, or how to get there either." I rolled over on my side. "And I'm the worst at actually committing to change. Like, Maxton, for instance. He's my type, he's always been my type, but I friend-zoned him from the get-go."

"I take it you kissed him again."

"How do you know that?"

He quietly groaned. "I could tell because you've changed your mind. This afternoon, you were still hesitant, but now you're agreeing with me and being fair—like you should be. I only wish it wasn't my dang idea!"

"Hey, I love that you can make me breathless and tingly, and I don't know—you're so intense and jump right to the heart of whatever we're talking about and pull out everything I refuse to say. I love that about you—how could I not love that?"

"But?"

"But , . . like I said before, Maxton has waited years for me to come around. He's kind, he's careful, and he's been crushing on me this whole time."

"Not to mention he's—what do you girls call his type—oh, yeah, he's hot and muscular and fun, too."

"I haven't really seen a lot of fun yet, but fun I could do." I needed something to distract me from the crazy in my life. After a few seconds, I said thoughtfully, "Anyway, I don't know who I am yet, but I'll figure it out. I'll become that person my mom always saw in me. Thanks for seeing me the way she did. It's given me hope." I got up on my elbow and glanced at the clock. It was nearly nine.

"Well, I guess I better head off. I've got a ton of homework to do. It was cool talking to you."

"Wait. Before you go," he said. "How was Clarise? Did she . . . Were you late after talking with Max? Was she mad?"

"Yeah, but you and Maxton were right—she's always mad. I'm not going to worry about it."

"Did you get in trouble?"

"Meh. The usual. Had to do some extra jobs."

"And?"

There were no secrets ever with Bryant. "And it was no big deal."

"Hey, I'm the guy you talk to now, remember? I'm the one who worries about you, and I'm here to take responsibility for whatever punishment you get because of my stupid ideas."

"Your ideas aren't stupid."

"What did Clarise say?"

I sighed and leaned back in my bed. "When I came in, she was waiting for me. She said she saw me pull up to the house with Maxton and then leave again, and she wanted to know where I went."

"Whoa. Max took you home and then took off with you again?"

"Yes. It's a long story. Anyway, none of this would've been a big deal except Jayda had waited for me after school to bring me home and then nearly missed getting back in time for basketball practice. She'd just gotten home before I did the first time, which is why Clarise was waiting for me at the door."

"So, Jayda didn't wait for you very long at the school."

"No, she probably saw me getting into Maxton's car and decided to race home and make a scene."

"Nice cousin."

"You have no idea."

"I'm beginning to."

He was, wasn't he? Actually, Bryant was fast becoming the only person who understood everything going on with me right now. It was strangely comforting and frightening all at the same time.

"So, did I put you through too much work?"

"Nah. Just the typical organizing a few closets, washing windows, straightening my cousins' rooms. That sort of thing. It's easy enough if I do it quickly. And for the record, you did not get me in trouble. I chose to hang out with Maxton."

"Did he know you were going to get in trouble when he pulled away?"

"Yeah, I sort of freaked."

"And his response was the same as mine? You're always in trouble, so what does it matter?"

"Pretty much. And you're both right."

"I'm sorry."

"For?"

"For forgetting you're not in a real family situation. When I get in trouble, my dad chews me out, but he listens because it's about something that matters to me. When you get in trouble, you become their servant."

I didn't say anything. I froze and allowed his words to sink in.

"What Maxton should've done—or any friend, including me—was walked in and taken the blame for making you late. My guess is, he drove up and dropped you off, and that can't work for you. He's got to be able to sweet-talk Clarise into letting him hang around and help you with whatever chores she gives you."

I couldn't believe what he was saying.

"Chances are, Clarise would back way down and not be so harsh on you, and in the end, she'd—"

"In the end, she could very well let me have it as soon as you—or any other boyfriend—left."

"Once," he said confidently. "I'd only let her get away with that once before I'd guarantee she never did that again."

His voice was so final, I had no clue what he was talking about. But the shouting of my name from upstairs meant I had to go.

"Indy! Come up here now!"

Dang it. "I gotta go. Speaking of the devil, Aunt Clarise is losing her mind. Bye."

"Let me know what happens."

After I hung up, I dashed up the stairs.

"I'm here!" I called as I rounded the corner. Clarise and my uncle were sitting down in the living room. My stomach clenched. This did not bode well.

"Have a seat, Indy," my aunt said as one thin leg bounced over the other.

My uncle didn't say a word as I sat on the plush loveseat she indicated. "What's up?" I asked, though my voice didn't come out as strong as I would've liked.

Clarise folded her arms. "Would you like to tell me what you and Maxton did after you left our driveway earlier?"

I glanced from one to the other. "Uh, we went and talked."

"And what else?" She flipped her brunette hair on her shoulder.

I had no idea where she was going with this. We didn't do anything else—we only talked. "That's it."

"Really? Are you sure about that?"

"Uh, yeah. Honestly, we were only gone a few minutes. We didn't have time to go on a date or anything."

"That's not what I'm talking about, Indy, and you know it." She looked as though she'd just caught me in some major lie.

I was going to be sick. I had no idea what Jayda or Kaitlyn had said to her, but it couldn't have been good.

My uncle coughed and said simply, "We received a phone call a few minutes ago that would imply otherwise."

Thankfully, I didn't have to wait long to hear what was going on. "Ms. Dillard said you and a boy in a red car parked outside her house and made out this afternoon."

"What?" Then I thought of the kisses and blushed. "Well, yes, we kissed. But we didn't make out. I promise!"

One slim eyebrow rose on Clarise's face, an indication that she was livid. "Do you have any clue how embarrassing that call was to get? Any at all?"

"I'm sorry. We left because we wanted to talk for a minute. I had no idea anyone was watching us."

"If you only wanted to talk, why did you stop in front of their house?"

My uncle stood and said, "I'm heading up to my office. Work out whatever you need to, Clarise. I can't think about this anymore."

"What?" She looked shocked. "Don't you want to help me figure this out? Something must be done. We can't let her go around acting like some . . . some *floozy* in front of the neighbor's house!"

His eyes met mine, and he shook his head. "Did you expect her to be anything else?"

The implication that I was brought up badly was not missed. I didn't know whether to cry or shout at them. All I knew for sure was that it hurt to hear stuff like that, and it was time it stopped. I stood up, my hands closing into fists. "What did you mean by that?"

"Never mind. You wouldn't understand." He gave my aunt a look that said, "Fix this." But I wasn't done—this conversation was most definitely not over.

"Is there something you'd like to tell me? Instead of standing there suggesting that my amazing mother raised me wrong, how about you act like a man of class and stop degrading the dead? My choices, my actions—they have nothing to do with my mother. My mom loved me and cared for me and worked her trash off providing for me, and she only said the nicest things about you both." I took a step forward and glared, not caring if they kicked me out of the house. I was done.

"And I'm sick to death of hearing how awful she was. How would you know? Did you ever come by and help us? Were you around at all? You have no idea how we lived or what I was taught—you only create your own filth in your minds and then spew it whenever something happens that you don't like."

I was on a roll, and suddenly, I couldn't stop. Everything I'd always wanted to say came out. I doubted if Bryant would ever consider me nice again. "I know you don't want me. I knew it the first day I came to stay with you. And you've made it extra clear ever since. I get it. I was this poor relation who ruined your vibe, but you didn't realize one thing. I was loved before I came here. I had the actual joy of belonging somewhere. I know the difference between this and what a kind and gentle soul is really like.

"I've done everything you've asked me to—everything. And that still isn't enough. Sure, my cousins can have dates and see people and have a life—but me? The girl their own age isn't allowed out of the house. I'm not even allowed to speak to my own boyfriend in front of the house, so we went a little bit away and talked. That's it. Other than one kiss, we talked. And now the whole world is over and my mom was a bad mother all because of what? Because I'm not treated equally in this house, because you want to guarantee that I forget what real love is? Is that it?"

Chapter 15

When my rant was over, I finally looked at them. Clarise had stood up too, probably so she wasn't the only one sitting. Her face looked as though someone had just released a pack of wild monkeys in her house and she had no idea what to do about it. Uncle David was pretty much as shocked as she was. Neither moved an inch.

I decided to stand there—even if it was awkwardly—until one of them said something. Storming off to my room in a huff would've been easier, but it wouldn't solve anything. I really wanted to know why I was treated so differently. "What will it take for you to see me as family?"

Clarise blinked. "Well, missy. That was definitely entertaining."

I put my hands on my hips. "It wasn't meant to be. I'm serious, and you should be too."

Uncle David was having none of it. "Listen here. You will be kind to my wife and respect us both while in this house, or you can find another place to live."

My aunt gasped, but didn't say anything.

"What is respect to you, Uncle David? What? Doing all the chores? Staying away during family activities and events? Hiding in the basement so your friends and coworkers don't see me? Basically living in an old storage closet and getting straight A's in school and having no friends, having no extracurricular activities, being a hermit until you ask me to come up and make dinner for you again? Is that respect? Then what part of that haven't I been doing? What more could you want from me?"

"You sound as though we treat you like a maid or something!" Clarise fumed. "Of all the ridiculous things to say to us! After all we've done, and how our lives had to change because of you!"

"Do you even hear yourself?" I asked. "Do you even realize what just came out of your mouth? I swear, you don't even know what you're saying."

"Says the girl who spends her free time humiliating us in front of the neighbors," Clarise hissed. "You will never have another boyfriend again, young lady! I will not have my niece pregnant before she's even graduated from high school!"

"How dare you say that? How dare you say something like that—it's insulting to me and to Maxton, who has only ever treated me with respect!"

"Enough!" David shouted. "Go to your room! We will decide when or how to punish you in the morning. And I promise you, it will be severe! And if you say one more word against either of us—if you continue to be an ungrateful, selfish brat—you'll be gone from this house tonight!" He walked up to me, his face red and his hand raised as if to hit me.

"David, no!" Clarise clung to his shirtsleeve, but my uncle was shaking now.

"Go! Leave now before you regret it!"

I ran. My feet pounded down the stairs and just managed to muffle the hammering in my ears as I bolted into my room and locked the door. As fast as I could, I began to shove whatever I could find into my bags. I had three old backpacks and a duffle. I didn't care what happened to me—I had to get out of there. They despised me. They hated my mom—and whatever stupid junk they made up about her, they obviously believed about me. Bigoted, mean, egotistical people who didn't know how to love anyone but themselves!

After I'd finished packing up the things in my dresser and my closet, including my few shoes and accessories, I glanced around the room. Aside from a few knickknacky things, I really didn't have that much. I took the photobook of my mom and all my school papers and awards that were shoved in my bottom door. I grabbed the few bits of artwork that I had and Mrs. Wiggins' toys that I'd made her and yeah—that was it.

There was nothing else to pack. So when they decided to kick me out, I could leave quietly and just go.

Reality began to sink in as I looked around my creepy room. A weird, tingly sensation began to replace whatever adrenaline I'd been using. My big mouth had ruined whatever chance I had with my family. Now they would never love me. Now they had the reasons they were looking for to think the worst of my mom. They would always blame her. I knew they would. And I could hardly breathe for being so stupid.

I set the last of my backpacks on the floor near my—no, Grandma's—bed and climbed on top of the blanket. I curled myself into a ball and stared at the wall in front of me. I had a quick thought to ask Grandma for help and then pushed it away. She was too old to take me in permanently. She might allow me in for a few hours, but as soon as she talked to Clarise and David, she'd side with them.

What was it about my mom that threatened her sister so much? What was it about me that made sure I wasn't treated like my cousins? Maybe they were right. Maybe I was an embarrassment and an offensive brat. I closed my eyes and took a deep breath, and then jumped when my phone chimed a text.

Good grief. It scared me to death. I decided I didn't want to talk to anyone right then, but when it went off a second time, I groaned and pulled it out to turn off the volume. The texts were from Bryant.

Hey, you okay? What did Clarise want?

Indy. Are you there?

I texted back. *Yeah, I'm here.*

You in trouble?

I stared at the phone and realized I'd never been in this situation before. I needed to tell someone I could very well be homeless in the next few hours. I started to call Bryant before I remembered he wasn't my boyfriend. So I did the right thing and texted Maxton. It was just after ten thirty.

Hey, are you up? I was hoping to talk. Could you call?

I waited and then got a text back.

Hi. Can't really talk right now. What's up?

Nothing. Well, nothing I wanted to talk about over text. *I'm okay,* I lied. *How are you?*

Haha. I was sleeping, probably dreaming about you, so you know that's good, right?

Sorry! I didn't realize I woke you up. So so sorry!

No worries. You sure there isn't anything?

My heart clenched, and I was so afraid, I really didn't know what to do. So I took a deep breath and told him. *You know, family drama. It's bad here. Probably the worst it's ever been.*

There. I pushed send and bit my lip. I wasn't good at asking for help. I really needed someone to tell me it was going to be okay.

A few seconds later, he replied. *Ugh. Sorry. Hey, well, tomorrow is a new day, right? Want to talk at lunch?*

Lunch? All at once, I felt like crying. So alone and lost and scared. He must be super tired. My face flushed in embarrassment for bothering him with my problems. I took a deep breath and gave a watery smile before answering. *Yeah, lunch would be cool. See you tomorrow.*

I sat up in my bed and brought my knees to my chest. As I wrapped my arms around my legs, I began to think and rock. Rock and think. I couldn't see a way out. Now that Uncle David had used the threat of kicking me out of the house, it wasn't going to go away. Even if tomorrow, everyone woke up and things were fine, they'd hold it over my head. And now that I'd had my stupid outburst and didn't keep my mouth shut and just take it—now they knew how I felt. Which meant they'd throw that at me every chance they got too. In one brief moment, I'd literally destroyed any chance of a normal life I could've had with them. Any chance of them growing to love me.

I'd completely managed to alienate my source of shelter, food, clothing—all of it. Why? Because I thought I was better than them? No. I winced and rocked. That wasn't it. I've never felt better than them—I only wished, or wanted, or needed to be treated fairly. That was it.

But what else did I expect? I never would've let them replace my mom anyway. Why did I think I deserved all these ridiculous rights, like boyfriends and movie nights and friends? I wasn't their daughter. Their duty wasn't to provide for me like my mom had. They took care of my needs. I shouldn't have expected gifts and favors like Jayda and Kaitlyn got. David and Clarise were *their* parents. I—I was someone they were watching for a few years. That's all.

Even though I was given new clothes at Christmas, and it was awkwardly done after they'd opened their presents and I was called up to get mine, I couldn't imagine a Christmas with no family at all. Or birthdays when I really was completely alone. But I'd just made sure I would never have a place to go to for the holidays.

I took a deep breath and wiped my eyes.

When I glanced at the phone I'd been clutching in my hand, I noticed six text messages. I hadn't even heard the thing chime. They were all from Bryant.

Hey. Are you in trouble?

Indy? Where'd you go?

Okay. I'm starting to get worried now.

Call me. Let's talk. I know we just talked, but let's talk again.

That's it. I won't be able to sleep now. I'm coming over. Hopefully you text before I get there and you tell me you're safe. That's all I need to hear. And also that your aunt didn't take your phone. Because if she took your phone, then all of this is really awkward. Doesn't matter. Gonna tell my dad I'm heading over there. Text me, dang it.

I'm here. Please come outside to the trampoline before I get busted for looking like a thug in your backyard.

Chapter 16

Holy cow. I quickly texted him back. *You're crazy. You know that?* All at once, I felt better. Not perfect, by any means—just better. Then I sent another text right afterward.

You can come to the side door, I'm pretty sure everyone else is upstairs in bed.

At least, I didn't hear anyone in the kitchen talking about how much they couldn't stand me living there.

I walked up to the door and opened it as he headed to the side of the house. I mimed for him to be quiet and then led him downstairs into the den. Bryant glanced in my room, then walked in. "Wait a minute," he whispered. "What's going on here? You look like you're packed up." I saw a flicker of something like panic go across his features.

"I . . . Let's sit down and talk." I pointed toward the couch.

"Okay. Hang on." He walked into my bedroom and then came back out. He was carrying the quilt from on top of my bed. "It's crazy cold down here, but you're probably used to it."

"Not as much as you'd think I'd be." It *was* cold. It was freezing in the den this late at night. "Thanks," I said as he wrapped both of us snugly on the smaller of the two couches.

"Okay. Now that you've given me a huge heart attack, want to explain what's going on?"

Words couldn't express how grateful I was to have him next to me. I leaned against his shoulder and spoke quietly.

"I really messed up. I mean, bad-bad."

I could feel his arm stiffen under my head. "What happened?"

"Clarise got a phone call from the neighbor down the street that implied Maxton and I parked and made out in front of her house this afternoon."

"Uh . . . did you?"

I groaned. "No. Well, we kissed, but no, we didn't make out. He did pull over in front of her house because I was freaking that I was going to get in trouble if we didn't go back. That's how that all happened."

"I'm assuming your aunt wasn't happy and chewed you out."

"Yes, her and Uncle David." I clenched my hands and tried to stop the shaking as the last hour came back to me. "And I don't know. You know how I get sometimes . . . well, I lost it. I basically told them off. Well—wait. No, first David implied that I am the way I am because of how I was raised, and *then* I told them both off. Because I was sick of it. I'm tired of hearing what a bad mom I had when they didn't even know her. They never hung around us or anything. They only assumed that because money was tight, I was raised to be rude and inappropriate or something."

"Are you kidding me? They talk bad about your mom?"

"All the time. And tonight, I snapped. Then Clarise said something about me getting pregnant, and I lost it again. Uncle David put his foot down and said he would kick me out if this disrespect continued, and he told me to leave and they'd decide in the morning what to do with me. But whatever they decide, he said it would be severe."

"So you came down stairs and started packing."

"Yeah."

He took a deep breath and wrapped me closer. "And then you realized that you had nowhere to go, and that you blew it and probably should've kept your mouth shut, and then sat down here and punished yourself for being rash?"

"How did you know?"

"Doesn't take a rocket scientist to figure out what you're thinking." His hand started to trail slowly up and down my quilt-covered arm. "I just want to know one thing. Did you tell them how unfair it is to be the one who does all the cleaning and gets left at home while your cousins actually get to live?"

I ruefully grinned and then winced. "Yes. It was awful. My filter was completely gone."

We sat in silence for a few minutes, and it was perfect. I needed to feel the presence of someone without all the muck of talking. I needed to unwind and think and pretend life was normal for a bit. Then Bryant broke the calm by asking quietly, "Indy, tell me honestly. Do you need a place to stay?"

"What?"

"I bet if I talked to my dad, he'd let you come and stay in our guest bedroom. I bet he wouldn't even hesitate."

I shifted a little to see him. Those dark eyes tugged at me. "Are you kidding?"

"No. I'm not. I've been thinking about it this whole time and I . . . I don't know what to do. Except getting you away from here."

"I can't believe you'd even offer something like that."

"Why?" One side of his mouth came up in an adorable grin. "You really have no idea how I feel about you, do you?"

"I don't know how many 'you's you used just then."

He chuckled and kissed my forehead. "Man, I miss you. You're not even gone and I can't stop thinking about you. I worry about you more than I have ever worried about anything before. It's kind of cool to know I can think about someone like this, someone who isn't me. You know what I mean?"

"It's probably learning how to adult."

He winked. "Probably." Suddenly he sat up and moved a few inches away. "Okay. I need to think, and that isn't going to happen while I'm staring at your gorgeous face. That confuses things—all I can think about is kissing you. And I can't do that because you've got a boyfriend."

Sure. Now *he wants to kiss me.* My heart began to speed up. "A boyfriend you told me to take."

"Don't remind me."

I laughed. Bryant's candid honesty and sweetness seriously undid me. "Fine. I'll move my tempting lips over here." I sat as far away as I could in the little loveseat.

He grumbled. "Maybe a little bit closer."

"Nope. Now out with it. What have you been thinking?" My heart was so much warmer than it'd been half an hour ago. It was unbelievable how sharing bad things with someone you loved changed your perspective on everything. I gasped. Loved. My eyes flew to Bryant's.

"What?" he asked. "Did you just think of something?"

I nodded, but there was no way I was going to tell him. "Anyway. It's no big deal. Tell me what you've been thinking. About staying with you."

Thankfully, that distracted him. "Oh. Yeah. Well, as I was sitting here, it dawned on me that your outburst—and their threats—aren't going to get any better. Since you said what we've all been wanting to say, that's really going to sting, and embarrass them. The problem with narcissistic people is that they believe they're always right. So if you start telling them they're wrong, you're basically throwing down the gauntlet. Then they'll stop at nothing to prove that you're the bad guy here and not them."

Whoa. I hadn't looked at it that way. "You think they're narcissistic?"

"Oh, classic case. Their daughters are perfect, but you're never allowed to be. Excuses to keep you in trouble. Not giving you natural freedoms. Not inviting you to stuff. Not even giving you a proper bedroom—the list goes on and on. There are some serious, actual abuse issues here. Stuff that's been bothering me for a long time."

"Abuse?" Suddenly, my warm heart hardened and dropped. "Are you kidding?"

"No, I'm not. It's definitely emotional, which is the most dangerous kind."

"How do you know all this stuff?"

He chuckled. "My dad's a psychiatrist. I would only have to tell him a fraction of what you've told me, and he'd have you removed from this house immediately."

My whole body went cold. "I had no idea."

Bryant nodded slowly. "It's not right, what they do to you. It's not healthy, either. And it's why I was determined that you have a somewhat normal life and a boyfriend and all that. What did Maxton say about tonight? Did you call him?"

"Well, I texted, but it was pretty late. So he said he'll see me at lunch tomorrow."

Bryant's eyebrows rose. "I think I need to have a talk with him."

"No, it's not his fault. After I realized I woke him up, I felt really bad, and I didn't want to bother him."

"Did he ask what you needed?"

"Yes, but I just told him it was bad here. Really bad. That's all."

"That should've been enough." He shook his head. And then he leaned forward and held my hand. "Indy, do you want to stay here? Or would you like to come to my house?"

"I can't imagine the trouble I'd get into if I left. They'd lose their minds."

"The choice wouldn't be theirs to make. My dad will vouch for you—and he'd vouch for your mom, too, if they tried to bring that up. There's no way they could hurt you again."

"Seriously?" I'd never imagined life outside of here. My eyes connected with his. "What if—what if things don't work out?"

"You mean, what if my dad doesn't want another teen girl in the house? Or are you talking about our friendship?"

"What if my aunt and uncle are right and I'm this horrible person who doesn't deserve anything? And you guys have me stay there a little bit, and then the truth comes out and you realize they were right?"

He sighed and gave a sad chuckle. "Indy, stop. I have no doubt in my mind that you're kind and caring and loving. The more I learn, the more I see, the better you become." He tugged on my hand and pulled me into him, wrapping the blanket more fully around us.

"Can I think it over for a few days before I decide?" I asked.

Those dark eyes probed. "Can I talk to my dad and let him know what's happening?"

"I . . . okay. I guess so."

"Hey, don't look like that." I had no idea what I looked like, but I loved that he snuggled me into him. He was so warm and strong and perfect. "I promise you, everything will be okay. You're going to be safe."

I nodded. "Uncle David was so mad at me. I shouldn't have said it. I should've just taken it."

"What are you talking about? You think it would've been better to hear lies about your mom?"

"No. But nothing I said changed their minds." I rested my head against his chest. "It wasn't worth it to defend her to people who never knew her."

"You shouldn't have to defend her at all."

"No. You're right."

He went quiet again for a few minutes and then said, "I really don't feel good about leaving you here tonight."

"You don't?"

I could hear his heartrate increase. It was fascinating. "No. I'd feel much better if you came home with me. Tomorrow, we can let my dad talk to your aunt and uncle, and we'll go from there."

"Do you think I'm in danger here?"

"I don't know. But every time I think of getting up and leaving you, something tells me not to. And it's beyond the normal 'I want-to-be-with-her-every-second' feeling. This one has a tinge of fear in it. Something urgent, telling me to protect you."

"My mom?" I whispered. I knew it was weird as soon as I said it, but to me, it made sense. I didn't want to explain it to anyone else, but I knew that if David and

Clarise had been abusing me, she would've been begging anyone to get me out of this house.

"Maybe. It's definitely intense enough to be from the other side—someone who loves and cares for you."

I think I died. Right then, my heart flipped for the hundredth time since knowing Bryant, and it settled warmly in my chest. He didn't mock the odd side of me, and that made him worth keeping forever. I moved back and melted into the most perfect guy I'd ever known.

Chapter 17

After a bit more useless arguing on my part, Bryant finally agreed to call his dad and get his opinion first. I hung out in the den while he went into the bedroom and made the late-night phone call. We decided on the bedroom for soundproofing reasons, and I opted to stay out in the den while I tried to make sense of my life.

How bad was it, really? Was Bryant right? Was I actually in the middle of some emotionally abusive junk? Is that why I'd had thoughts of suicide, because my family wasn't capable of holding and loving a little girl in mourning?

I'd never even gotten so much as a hug from my aunt. And it wasn't until that moment that reality hit me. I imagined being given a very scared, lost little ten-year-old girl and then placing her in a cold, creepy basement, never including her, teaching her not to question it. Telling her daily she didn't deserve it.

I wrapped Grandma's blanket around me and curled up into the side of the couch. I missed my mom. And it was times like this when I really wished she were there to tell me what to do.

I must've dozed because the next thing I knew, Bryant was gently rousing me.

"Hey, Sleeping Beauty. I talked to my dad."

I blinked. "Sorry. I didn't realize I'd fallen asleep."

He grinned. "You've been through a lot today. I bet you're exhausted."

"No, no. I'm fine," I lied through a huge yawn. "So, what did your dad say?"

"Well, after I told him everything, he was as concerned as I thought he'd be. He's also very relieved you allowed me to tell him." Bryant knelt down in front of the couch. "What I didn't realize, though, is that now my dad knows what's happened here, he's legally obligated to turn this over to Child Protective Services."

"What? Are you sure?"

"Yeah, he could actually lose his license if he doesn't. But the good thing is, you won't have to be here anymore. This isn't healthy. My dad is going to help you get into a healthier place both physically and mentally."

All at once, I felt like I was on some reality TV show and had been taken away from everything I knew. But this was my life, and honestly, I couldn't believe it was bad enough that the state had to be called on my aunt and uncle. It wasn't like they beat me or something. "This is so weird."

"I know. I'm sorry. And I promise, no one at school needs to know anything. We'll keep it private."

School? I groaned when I thought about seeing my cousins. "I don't know. I can't do this. Jayda and Kaitlyn are going to flip."

"This isn't about them anymore. It's about you."

I took a deep breath.

"By the way, my dad says he has no problem letting you to stay with us. He's completely certified to take in foster kids, and fostering you would be a real honor."

"He said all that?"

"Yep." He shifted to his knees. "Now, the real issue—what to do with you. My dad said that as a professional, understanding the situation as he does—since he trusts me—he feels the same way I do. You're not safe. And you need to come home with us tonight."

I shook my head. It was all too much. "I don't think they'll hit me or anything."

Bryant took a deep breath. "No, but they might lock you in your room or something."

I thought of all the times I'd been locked in that very room. Sometimes days at a time during the summer, only to be let out for bathroom breaks. I softly gulped. "So, is locking someone in their room abuse?"

Bryant's eyebrows rose. "Right. You've said enough." He pulled me up. "I'm getting the bags. You grab whatever stuff you need, and I'll meet you by the side door. We're leaving now."

"Wait. You didn't answer me."

"I didn't need to. If they've locked you in your room for being a normal kid, what will they do now? Tomorrow morning won't be pretty. If you don't come home with me tonight, I'll be staying down here in the basement to escort you to school."

"No way. Clarise would lose her mind. She'd call the cops and everything."

He smirked. "Bring the cops. I'd love to tell them everything I know."

Bryant Bailey had to be the hottest guy I'd ever known. Or would ever meet. "Aren't you afraid of the cops?"

"I'm positive that what I have against her is way more than anything she'd say against me." He put his hand on my shoulder. "Anyway, this is ridiculous because you're coming with me."

A new fear began to grow inside me. Not of Bryant or his family—I knew they were right—but more of the reality that things would never be the same again. And I had no idea what to expect. Which I guess was why I balked at the idea to begin with—I wasn't ready for change. I took a deep breath to calm my nerves. Sometimes, you need to close your eyes and leap.

Without saying a word, I walked past Bryant and into the small downstairs bathroom. I grabbed my towel, robe, and toothbrush, and then I pulled out the makeup bag under the sink and filled it full of all my toiletries. Afterward, I took a really long look at the girl in the mirror staring back at me.

She was tired, but hopeful, and I was surprised to find a little bit of sparkle in her eyes. As if I was actually more excited than I realized. One thing was for certain—it sure beat feeling like I was all alone again. I tilted my head to the side and said, "You've got this." My eyes grew watery and it was hard to see myself, but I took another deep breath. "It's time. This is about you. It isn't about them anymore."

And then, before I lost my nerve, I followed a fully loaded Bryant up the stairs and out the door toward his waiting car.

Chapter 18

"Welcome, Indy!" Dr. Bailey greeted me as I came through the front door of Bryant's huge house. He was a tall, handsome man, clean shaven with dark hair like Bryant's, but graying at the temples. His smile was large and exposed two dimples. He wore jeans, socks, and a T-shirt. It looked like I hadn't woken him up with my nonsense, and I was grateful for that.

"Thank you." I smiled shyly at him and then turned to Bryant and whispered, "You didn't tell me you lived in a castle." I was pretty sure we were walking on marble tiles. The whole expanse of the entryway into a large room with a swooping staircase was done in ornate swirled tiles.

He chuckled. "It's big, but it isn't *that* big, thank goodness."

"I won't bother you two," Dr. Bailey interrupted. He said to Bryant, "I'll let you show her around. Stick to the main part of the house or she may get a little confused at first."

"Lost. The word you're looking for is lost," Bryant said.

"Yeah, well, keep her close. Go ahead and put her in the guest bedroom across from yours for the next week or so." He turned to me. "I want you to feel as comfortable as you can, so I hope you don't mind being close to him—he is a boy, and you know they stink sometimes."

"Dad!"

I laughed when Dr. Bailey wiggled his eyebrows and said, "In a while, when you're ready, I'll move you to the girls' wing of the house. There are a few guest bedrooms over there for you to choose from. Bryant will help you get settled. I have a feeling it's going to be a lengthy day tomorrow."

"Sorry," Bryant whispered as we headed up the stairs and down a long wide hallway. "I don't usually tell people about my house. They tend to freak, or beg to throw parties here, which would never happen. It was my mom's thing. She'd always loved the houses in Europe. She went to a few universities over there, and so when my dad married her, his dream was to surprise her with a house like that of her own. And as you can see, they were both quite happy."

I lost count of the small sofas and random fancy high-backed chairs along the way. "Why do you guys have so many places to sit? Do you use them?"

Bryant looked around and laughed. "I don't know why. We hardly ever sit on them. I'd forgotten they were there until you mentioned it. I think it's more of a European decorating thing."

We passed a few closed doors and some incredible artwork before Bryant stopped in front of a dark carved door. "Here we are." He opened it, and I tried to keep my cool by not gasping.

The room had a large four-poster canopy bed with a thick comforter and a dozen fun accent pillows in blue and green. There was a pretty white dresser and green-and-blue floral curtains, a rug, and another door that led to a beautiful bathroom. "Um, I think this room is a little too nice." I felt bad even sleeping in it. It looked like it belonged on a movie set.

Bryant chuckled. "Nah, that's just my mom. She loved detail, especially when it came to the guest bedrooms." He dropped my bags on the floor near the nightstand by the bed. "I'll show you my room, and you'll see what I mean."

We walked across the hall into a bedroom that was nearly twice the size of mine. It too had a four-poster bed, but that's where the similarities ended. Bryant had opted for a dark-blue comforter.

"I love the pictures on your wall." I walked in and studied some of the abstract modern art he had up. I looked closer. "These are originals. How fun!" They were brightly painted with splashes of different colors. They created shapes with no pattern or consistency, just something fascinating to look at.

"Thanks. My mom bought them from a friend when she was overseas. They never really matched her décor, but I loved them, so she let me put them up here in my room." He turned around and pointed to a few more behind us. "There are six paintings altogether."

"So your mom's family had a lot of money?" I winced as soon as it came out of my mouth. "Never mind. Scratch that."

"No, it's okay. My dad makes money as a psychiatrist, but not this much. My parents both come from influential families in Scottsdale, but they wanted to escape the heat of both family life and the valley and came up here to settle." He crumpled up some trash that was on his bed and threw it at a mini basketball hoop attached to his wall. Two of the three papers made it into the waiting trash can below. The other one bounced off the rim and onto the floor. "We have family here all the time. Mom knew we would—especially during the summer, when it's much cooler up here. When they were designing the house, my parents added enough room for both their families to come. It's only about seven guest bedrooms, but it does seem to add up. Plus the fact that there are another five bedrooms just for me, my sisters, and Dad, and the study, parlors, library—er, it's a bit much, I know. But you get used to it after a while."

"Wow." Clarise would kill for this house.

On the drive here, I'd almost fallen asleep, but now, I was too wound up even to think about hitting my pillow. It was nice to be welcomed into this extraordinary place, but I still couldn't stop feeling uneasy as I wondered what was going to happen tomorrow. I watched as Bryant continued to clean up his room by using his basketball hoop. I had to admit it was pretty genius.

"So, what do you think Clarise will do when she realizes I'm not there?"

Bryant stopped shooting hoops. "Are you worried? You're probably sick to death, aren't you?"

"I'm a little queasy—yeah. Just anxiety and . . . hoping I did the right thing, I guess." I should have gone to my room and let him get to bed, but I didn't want to be alone just yet.

"I'm sorry." He grabbed a few books from his dresser and started heading toward my room. "I promise, you did the right thing by coming here. I wish my house was more normal and more comfortable for you. At least you're with friends now—and it helps me to know you're safe."

He talked to me through the door while I used the bathroom to change into my pajamas, brush my teeth, and wash my face, and then he helped dump a ton of pillows from the bed as I crawled under the thick covers. "Hey. You're gonna be okay. I can't imagine what's going on in your mind right now, but we'll figure this out together."

I reached up and grabbed his hand. "Thank you."

Bryant searched my eyes and then whispered, "How did I get lucky enough to find you?"

I rolled my eyes and grinned—only because I knew I was about to ruin the moment. "You killed my cat."

He looked up at the ceiling and shook his head. "I will never live it down—ever."

"Nope."

"Is it okay to want to kiss a friend who's in bed, or is that a bit creepy?"

"The friend you just rescued from her abusive home, who's now staying in the room across from you? Yeah, it's a tad creepy. This is more the time to bring up things like security, safety—things that won't create butterflies."

He leaned over. "So you're saying my kisses would give you butterflies?"

I giggled, unclasped my hand from his, and pushed against his mouth as he lowered it toward me. "Go away, Bryant. I already snuggled with you earlier today. You don't even want me as a girlfriend, so you have no one to blame but yourself."

He kissed my palm, and a million crazy tingles shot from my hand to my elbow. "Fine. I see how it is. Reject the guy who saved you." He pouted, turned around, and started to walk away.

"I don't care how slow you walk—you're not getting kisses from me while I'm in this bed. It's weird."

He turned around and grinned. "So, are you saying I can kiss you other rooms in the house?"

Good grief. "Go to sleep, Bryant. If you're lucky, I won't murder you in your sleep, and you'll actually wake up tomorrow."

"You would never hurt this face. I'm much too good-looking. You need this face. The world needs this face."

I laughed. "And don't forget to close the door on your way out."

"You're never going to let up, are you?"

"Somebody has to put you in your place!"

He laughed and whispered, "I love you." Then he shut the door.

My heart started to beat frantically, and no matter how hard I tried, I couldn't keep Maxton's face in my mind. Instead, this dark-haired, dark-eyed, monstrously good-looking prince kept coming into focus. He loved me. After all these years, it felt incredibly wonderful to be loved again.

I curled up in the luxurious covers and dreamed of life and new beginnings.

Chapter 19

"What do you mean, the state has ordered Indy back to her aunt's house? I won't allow it! I don't care who the legal guardian is—she's sixteen years old, and able to choose for herself where to be interviewed."

I clenched my hands in Dr. Bailey's study and watched as he paced the floor, talking to the police officer on the phone. His brown leather shoes matched the leather of the furniture and the stained bookshelves.

"I don't care if they have ten lawyers and want to have all interviews done at their house. It's illegal, and you know it!"

Bryant walked over to the chair where I sat and squeezed my hand.

"It's going to be okay. The cops are just trying to please everyone, but Dad knows the law. He won't let your aunt and uncle get away with anything illegal."

"You and I both recognize you don't have the rights to pick up this girl and take her there. She wants all the interviews to be held at Child Protective Services. This is a stupid ploy to stall, and it's wasting valuable time. I'm calling the case manager back, and we'll come to an agreement. As her doctor, I assure you that no matter where the private interview is held, nothing will change. And for the moment, she has chosen to live here."

Bryant nudged me over and sat on the arm of my chair. "It sounds like your aunt and uncle are worried they're going to get in trouble, so they're trying to slow the process to give them more time to get their story straight. My dad has worked on hundreds of cases like this and has protected kids in way worse situations than yours. Once a lawyer is involved, they call the cops and try to write up a report. It's a scare tactic. Without court orders, the cops aren't going to get involved. They just call to see if their badges can sway people to get along. What the lawyer is trying to do isn't legal. He and my dad and the cops all know it—which is why he figures they're just trying to stall."

Everything was confusing. "Does it matter where they interview me? Do Clarise and David have any rights?"

"No. Your interview will be privately done, no matter what. My dad will see to that. A lot of the time, abusers try to be there so they can intimidate the one being questioned, but they can't be there. It's useless, but they'll still use a lawyer and try it anyway. Just in case someone doesn't know the law."

"What are they going to ask me?"

He shook his head. "I'm not certain. But I know it won't be anything too scary."

"Are you sure I have to go through this?" I wished I was back in bed, or at school, or anywhere but here.

"You need to get evaluated for my dad to be granted custody. It's procedure. And it protects those parents who have been wrongfully accused of something. The whole system is set up to help. It doesn't always have the best reputation, but I promise, it'll be okay in your case."

That morning, it had been decided pretty early on that neither me nor Bryant would be going in to school. Dr. Bailey—Jeff, as he had asked to be called—moved several of his appointments to the evening, and then spoke to me for nearly two hours before contacting CPS and talking with the case manager. He'd also been on the phone with Clarise and the city cops more than once to let everyone know I was safe.

"It's almost one. Are you hungry?" Bryant asked. "Do you think you could eat something?"

I was too nervous to eat breakfast, and now I was starving. "Yes." Besides, it would give me something to do besides worrying about stuff I had no control over.

I followed Bryant through a labyrinth of rooms until we came to the large gourmet kitchen that would be any chef's dream. I'd been there earlier that morning and met his sisters as they were heading off to school, but I honestly had no idea how to get there again without following Bryant.

He walked up to a beautiful antique-looking white cupboard and opened it to reveal a huge fridge. I couldn't believe it'd been hidden away in there. "That's amazing."

"What?" He glanced around as I walked up to it. The thing looked about twice the size of any refrigerator I'd seen. Maybe even three times.

"I love how it's made to look like a big cupboard."

"Oh, yeah. My mom's dream fridge, too." He started to pull out a bunch of different foods. "Are sandwiches okay? We've got a lot of sliced meat and cheese."

"Sandwiches work." I helped him by taking the mustard and mayo from the door, though the mustard seemed a bit light. I opened it up and peered inside. "I think you're out."

Bryant pulled out the bread and lettuce and then shut the door. "Here, let me see." He took the container and shook it. "Yep. Looks like we'll have to do without. Can't believe someone put it back in there empty."

I don't know why, but I started to laugh. Maybe it was good to know they were still a normal family. "I'm a little shocked," I teased. "I can't believe that with this huge castle and these incredible rooms and everything, you have an empty condiment bottle in your fancy fridge."

"Whatever." He chuckled. "I'm sure if my mom were here, this never would've happened."

I began to spread mayo onto my bread. "I don't know if I can actually eat a sandwich without mustard. My hopes are completely dashed." I pulled off a few leaves of lettuce and washed them in the sink while Bryant opened the meat and cheeses.

"How big are we making these?" I asked as I eyed at least six different types of meat and three cheeses.

"Well, I don't know what you like, so I brought it all out so you can choose. See? I'm being a gentleman."

"Are you two already fighting like siblings?" Dr. Bailey—er, Jeff—asked as he came into the kitchen.

"Already fighting?" I laughed. "I've been wanting to kill Bryant since we first met."

Bryant finished making his sandwich and took a bite. "So true."

Jeff made quick work of the ingredients and shoveled a sandwich together. It must be a guy thing—I'd barely added a lettuce and a piece of cheese to mine. Bryant's dad grabbed a plate and sat his sandwich on it. "Well, as long there's no blood on the carpet, I guess I can't complain." He walked out of the kitchen with Bryant trying not to choke with laughter.

• • •

"I like your dad." I grinned and placed a few pieces of meat and the other slice of bread on top.

"Most people do. He's pretty cool."

I nodded and took my first bite of heaven. I don't know if it was because I was in a new environment, or that for the first time, I could eat without being worried what Clarise would say about how I chewed my food, or the amount I'd taken, or the mess on the counter. I took another bite. It was probably the latter.

Bryant dug through a different cupboard and brought out some barbeque-flavored chips, then went searching for plates. "Want to sit on the little table in here?" He walked over to the kitchen nook.

"Sure." I grabbed a couple of glasses, filled them up with water, and then headed over to him.

As we ate, I had to ask the one question that'd been plaguing me since I got there. "Is it hard, having so many reminders of your mom everywhere?" I'd never had to face that, since I moved as soon as she'd died. But I couldn't imagine what it must be like to be constantly reminded of her.

Bryant shrugged. "I don't know. At first, maybe. Now it's sort of good. I like to think that a part of her will always be here. And even years down the road, we can still enjoy what she left behind."

I sat the rest of my sandwich down as my heartache settled for a bit.

"What's wrong?" he asked.

"Nothing, really. Just got sad for a second."

"That's the hardest part about losing someone—those waves of sadness hit, and you have no idea what triggered them or how long they'll last. Makes it awkward sometimes because one second, you're having a blast, and the next, you're close to tears."

I was definitely close to the tears part. "Yeah. I can't even figure out why."

"Well, we were talking about having so many memories of my mom around—are you sad that your family sold everything, and you don't have the connection we do?"

"I wish someone had thought about me. I wish they had seen a picture or jewelry box or dish of my mom's and thought, 'Indy would love this one day.'" I sighed and plucked at a chip on my plate. "They thought I was too young. They didn't even give me a voice. No one asked me if I'd like something. I didn't even know I was moving until I was."

"Hey." He leaned over and squeezed my hand. "We'll figure it out, okay? I promise. We'll piece together your mom's favorite things and start a Cindy collection."

My eyes met his. "Why are you so sweet?" He wasn't like anyone else I knew. "Honestly, I swear you're not a teenage guy. You're not."

"Nah. You figured me out. I'm a three-thousand-year-old alien come to earth disguised as a junior."

I grinned.

"Hey, at least you smiled." Bryant ate a few chips and then answered thoughtfully, "You know, I'm not sure. I mean, we've talked about this before, and I really think it has to do with losing my mom. Seeing the world in a series of important moments. Life isn't something to ignore and zoom past—it's a chance to take each moment you can with those around you."

He stood up and took his plate from the table, returning with a bag of cookies. "I figured out a long time ago that I was supposed to learn something new from each person I met. That their input in my life—whether bad or good—taught me how to go forward. I can't risk missing one of those teaching moments—like ignoring how you were being treated." His eyes grew a bit misty as he continued. "Last night, when you didn't text back, I knew it was something. And it scared me. Maybe other people can leave stuff like that alone without acting on their gut instincts, but not me. I knew you'd think I was crazy, but I didn't care."

He ran his hands through his hair and totally messed it up. "I love you, Indy." Shaking his head, he spoke before I could. "I know it's weird for me to say this now—I know it's considered stupid or whatever—but I can't take not knowing if you're safe. And the stupidest thing I did—since I'm confessing anyway—was trying to put some distance between us. Seriously, what is wrong with me, telling you to get another boyfriend?"

"Stop," I said quietly. "I admit, I was a little peeved that you said you wanted me to give Maxton a chance. But I saw beyond myself to the people who'd already been helping me and I didn't even realize it."

"He's a good guy."

"He's really awesome."

Bryant rubbed his head again and closed his eyes. "And you guys make a really good couple."

"We probably do." I tugged on his arm. "But I'm not going to stay with him, dork."

Chapter 20

"Wait. What? Why not?" Bryant's face was too funny.

Because I love you too. Except I was too scared to say it, so I said, "Because I can't lie to him. And it'll get seriously awkward once he knows I'm staying here with you at your huge palace."

"Oh."

"Though I did promise to go to one of his wrestling matches. I feel like such an awful friend—all these years, he's been wrestling, and I've never gone once."

"So when is his next one?"

"Saturday."

"And you want to go?"

I messed with some crumbs on my plate. "Yeah. Is that bad of me? To go even though we're breaking up?"

"Well, that depends. When are you planning to break up with him?"

"Probably soon."

"So, before the match?"

"Yes."

He nodded. "Okay, I guess that's better than breaking up with him *at* the match." He chuckled and then looked a little sad. "Actually, getting dumped is never fun, no matter when it happens."

"So, are you saying I shouldn't break up with him?"

"No. I'm saying it isn't going to be easy. Period."

I sighed. "Here's the thing. If I prolong it like you wanted me to and give him an actual chance, wouldn't it be a worse breakup down the road than getting it over with early?"

"Not necessarily. To some guys, it would seem like you tried to give them a chance, that you were willing to make it work. And if you dump them after a couple of days, it'll be like you didn't think they were worth it."

"Great. Thanks. Now you're making me feel really bad."

"You're right. You're right. I'll keep my mouth shut."

Just then, Dr. Bailey walked back into the kitchen. "Okay. The case worker is willing to meet with you in about forty minutes." He glanced at me. "Does that sound good? We'll have to leave in almost fifteen minutes."

I looked over at Bryant. "Yes. I guess so."

Jeff put his hands on his hips and sighed. "Great. Took all morning, but I think we've finally gotten it sorted it."

"Will my aunt and uncle be there too?"

"No. This is your chance to speak up and share whatever you'd like without worrying about what they'd think."

"And then after I do?"

"Usually, they'd remove you from the home immediately, but that's already happened. We'll probably have to go to a hearing on your behalf—you won't need to be there—where I share my side and your case worker will share her side and together, we'll go against your aunt and uncle's attorney to gain full custody of you."

"What if you don't win?"

"Oh, I'll win. Don't worry about that."

"Yes, but . . .? Just in case you don't get custody, does that mean they will? Do I go back to live with Clarise?"

"No. Never again. With your testimony and what you've been through, you'd go to live with a foster family if it didn't work out with me."

I didn't want to get my hopes up. "But I've never been hit—I know you say it's emotional abuse, but I think it'd need to be more serious than that."

"Indy." He put his hand on my shoulder. "You have to remember that neglect is also considered abuse. After speaking with you today, they'll be able to come up with several examples of mistreatment."

"Will something happen to my aunt and uncle?"

He shrugged. "Honestly, I have no idea what the judge will decide. I know that in extreme cases, people have gone to jail, but that's not any of our concern. What we need to do is make sure you start counseling right away and get you healthy and healing."

He looked over at Bryant. "I know you've got feelings for Indy, but I'm going to ask you to cool it for right now. She's as confused as she'll ever be and we need to treat her as friends, as family, until she can balance and heal properly. Then, if you guys decide you'd like to do a few things together, you will go very slowly and treat her with the utmost respect. Do you understand?"

Bryant looked down, and I swore I could see him blushing. "Dang it." He grinned when he glanced back up. "You're killing me, Dad."

"You'll live, I'm sure." Jeff then looked over at me. "You're going to have a lot of emotions flood through you in the next couple of months. That's normal—it's okay. Whenever you'd like to talk, please come to me. We'll get this all worked out."

Then he pulled me up out of the chair, gave me an enormous hug, and said, "Welcome to the family."

It felt good to be hugged, but I thought I'd least try to make Dr. Bailey see reason as I stepped back. "But what if I like Bryant and think I'm falling in love with him already?"

"You too, eh?" Jeff grinned and patted my back, all fatherly. "Well, here's the deal. How about we see how well this works, and then in a couple of months, we go from there?" He looked at us both. "Come on, guys. You've got to work with me on this one."

"Okay, I promise to be good and view Indy as a friend for now."

Dr. Bailey looked at me. Did he expect me to speak too? "Um, I promise not to kiss him."

Bryant burst out laughing. And his dad and I had to join in.

"What?" I asked over a few chuckles. "What else am I supposed to say?"

"Nothing." Jeff looked at me with a new light in his eye. "Nothing at all. In fact, I think you may be exactly what this family has needed for a very long time."

I don't know what came over me, or why that particular statement affected me, but right then, I burst into tears. Happy, relief-filled tears. Dr. Bailey and Bryant hugged me, and I think they shed a few tears with me.

Then Jeff said, "It's nice to finally belong, isn't it?"

I had no words. I just nodded.

He continued, "You will always be welcome here. You're family now—whether you stay here or not. You are always welcome back. You will be loved."

"Thank you." It was all I could say. "Thank you."

***

Much later that night, after I'd spoken with Child Protective Services and Bryant and his sisters and I were taking a much-needed movie break, I got a text from Maxton.

Hey, I noticed you weren't at school today. Is everything all right?

I didn't even know how to answer him, or where to begin. I stared at the phone for a good five minutes before I answered back.

Yes, everything is good now. I moved out. I'd love to tell you about it. Too long for text. When can we talk?

He responded quickly. *I can't tonight, but I should be able to tomorrow. Will you be at lunch?*

I didn't care how private our lunch table was—there was no way I'd be telling him at school. I'd prefer somewhere more private. *Could you come to my new house after school?*

Are you going to break up with me? Is this why you keep wanting to talk?

Bryant had been pretending he didn't notice that I'd been texting someone, but I nudged him with my arm and showed him the phone. "What do I do?" I whispered.

I mean, I wasn't going to break up with Maxton right then. I really wanted to let him know what had happened to me—I mean, it was kind of epic. However, I didn't want to lie either, since I had every intention of breaking up with him later. Gah. So, was that why he wasn't talking to me?

He was afraid of getting dumped? Dang it! I'd needed him the night before.

"Well, that bites," Bryant answered quietly. Neither of us wanted to disturb the others watching the movie.

"Do I tell him yes?"

He shrugged. "Yeah, I guess. But if you leave it at just yes, he'll never hear the rest, and then really be left out of everything. He deserves to know. Hang on." Bryant pulled out his phone and said, "Give me his number. I'll text him. Maybe that will help out a little."

"What? Are you kidding me? No. You're not texting him. I can do it."

"Indy, stop being stubborn and give me the number."

"What are you going to say?"

"You've gotta learn to trust me."

"Shh!" his littlest sister hissed. "You guys are being loud."

I couldn't remember if she was eleven or twelve, but her panda and red-striped jammies were adorable on her. I refused to fight in the midst of such cuteness. I handed him the phone and watched as he punched in the number.

Hey, this is Bryant Bailey. Wanted to give you a heads-up, since you know Indy. Her aunt and uncle are being investigated by the state for child abuse, and she's staying here with me for the time being. If you'd like to come by and see her, you are welcome anytime. Thanks.

He showed it to me before he pushed send. After I agreed, he asked, "Happy?"

"Yes." It was much better than what I would've said.

He chuckled and wrapped an arm around me. "That's because you're a girl."

"Shh!" His fourteen-year-old sister hushed us.

"Roni, you have seen this movie a hundred times. Do you really need us to be quiet?"

"Gah!" His youngest sister looked like she was going to throw a pillow at him. Her dark braids seemed to huff with her.

I tried to muffle my laughter. "So, are these the family movie nights I've been missing all these years?"

He gave me a rueful grin. "Pretty much. Popcorn, fighting, and movies we've seen hundreds of times."

I couldn't think of a more perfect way to spend a school night. The warm glow in my heart seemed to expand all the way to the top of my head and down to the tips of my toes. Nothing felt better than that. Nothing.

Just before bed, Maxton texted again.

Sorry to put you on the spot like that. Bryant texted me and told me what happened. We have a lot to talk about. I'll come over to the Baileys' house after school tomorrow. If that works?

I responded pretty quickly. *Thanks. Yes, that works. Bryant's dad is working my case, so it's complicated, but I probably won't be at lunch tomorrow again.*

No worries. We'll catch up. Goodnight.

Chapter 21

Bryant and I were kind of in limbo—and I don't mean relationship-wise. I mean with school. Dr. Bailey was still debating with the caseworker on whether or not I should attend the same high school as my cousins, or move to a charter school nearby. Before he'd even asked Bryant what he thought, Bryant volunteered to move over with me to keep some sort of consistency going, which I was really grateful for.

After more long talks with Jeff in his study—and more specifically, about how I was treated by Jayda and Kaitlyn—it became apparent by the end of the day that I was not to attend the high school again. Which sort of stressed me out and relieved me all at the same time. I'd had no idea how much my life would change when I'd first agreed to head out the door with Bryant.

Dr. Bailey then spent a significant time on the phone with the charter school and their counselor before hanging up and announcing Bryant and I had the rest of the week off and would be enrolling next Monday. I admit it, I sort of cried then too. And we all hugged once more, standing outside of his study.

It'd been a long couple of blurry-eyed days for me, but there was so much healing and relief. It was nice not to have to be the one to make all the decisions. That feeling, that I was actually being taken care of, was simply wonderful.

By the time Maxton rang the doorbell, my eyes were already swollen, and I'd forgotten he was coming.

"Hi!" I smiled a little too brightly and ran my fingers through my hair. "How are you?"

Maxton stood in the doorway for a minute, just looking around. Then he asked, "You want to talk outside?"

Yeah, the house was a bit much. I'd almost forgotten that part.

"Let me get my coat." I grabbed it from a hidden closet near the door and joined him on the porch. "Hi," I said again. "Let's head over here."

I walked him to the side of the house. It had a pretty little garden that probably looked gorgeous in the spring, with a swing that Margo, Bryant's twelve-year-old sister, had shown me that afternoon. We sat down together and began to rock.

"So, new digs, huh?" He smiled. "This place is crazy."

"Yeah, it is. You have no idea."

Maxton took a deep breath and turned toward me. "I really don't fit anywhere."

"Why do you say that?"

"I just don't—you have Bryant now, and I'm stupid for not trying for you sooner."

Right. He'd brought up the topic of us without asking how I was doing first. I admit, it kind of hurt. Especially since he'd been so kind to me all this time—I thought his first priority was me. I sighed. It was selfish of me to dump such a history on Maxton anyway. He knew some of what had happened to me, but he really had no clue. I'd kept most of it hidden away. It wasn't until Bryant that anyone learned the truth.

After I didn't respond, he added, "Look, you're an awesome girl. I've known it since we were in grade school together. You're funny, you're tough, and you're quick. Getting to spend the last few years with you was a dream come true for me. It really was. You made it worth going to school every morning."

"Seriously?"

"I've had the biggest crush on you forever."

"Thank you." I smiled, reached over, and took his hand in mine. "You cared for me and were a friend to me when I had no one. On some of my deepest, hardest days, I looked forward to eating lunch and chatting with you. You made me feel normal, and made me forget how bad my life was."

"Good. I'm glad, though I had no idea you were suffering that much. Did you really get removed because of abuse?"

I looked out toward the large field to the side of the house. "Yeah, but I'm safe now. And I can already feel myself beginning to heal from everything." I glanced at Maxton and tried to relieve a bit of his confusion. "Dr. Bailey is my psychiatrist. He's the one who turned my aunt and uncle in. He's working with me, helping me with my mom's death and the unfairness of the last six years or so. And he says he'll help me with Mrs. Wiggins too."

"That's cool. He sounds like a really nice guy. I mean, looking at this place, I wouldn't want to like him, you know? But he seems decent."

"And I'm not going to Flagstaff High anymore. I'll be attending the charter school."

"I kind of figured that already."

"Found out today."

"So, I guess that means I don't have to eat nasty cafeteria food anymore."

I laughed and nudged him. "That alone should prove you deserve a medal."

"It's amazing what a guy will go through to hang with the girl he likes." His large hand gently squeezed my much-smaller one.

Then it hit me. I had the perfect excuse we'd both been sitting here hoping for. "So, Dr. Bailey doesn't think I should have a boyfriend right now. He says I've got too much emotional stuff happening that I need to address before I get caught up in a relationship."

"Wow. So, you really are going to break up with me?"

I nodded slowly. "Yep. Doctor's orders."

We were silent for a little while as the swing moved back and forth. It was calming. And a sort of perfect way to end our complicated relationship.

After a few more minutes of chatting, Maxton said he had to go. So we hugged, one final big bear hug, and I shed a few tears when I wasn't quite ready to let him go. Then he left. Even though I knew we'd keep in touch, I also remembered what Bryant had said—Maxton was never going to be the same again. And he wasn't. We weren't. But it was okay. It was time.

I needed to find me, and that meant being fine with moving on.

***

As luck would have it, Jeff wasn't just good at his job—he was *really* good. Between his testimony and the state's, my aunt and uncle decided not only to relinquish custody of me, but to pay me almost three hundred thousand dollars in restitution. Three hundred thousand dollars that Dr. Bailey's snooping found belonged to my mom's life insurance claim. My aunt and uncle had taken it, as my legal guardians, to raise me, but since they hadn't done that and instead sold all of our belongings, they agreed to pay an additional two hundred thousand to make up for the missing assets and any emotional trauma it could've caused me.

I couldn't touch more than twenty-five grand until I turned eighteen, but holy cow! I was loaded. What teenager needed that much money anyway?

Jeff promised he'd set me up with his personal wealth manager on how best to invest the money to get the greatest return. Thankfully, I had such awesome people in my life now. Jeff believed that if I only used what I needed for college and bought a nice used car now, the financial advisor could easily triple or quadruple the money by the time I turned twenty-five.

Funny thing was, I never wanted the money. Never even thought I'd have any. I only wanted to belong. Now I had both.

That summer, after I took my much-needed driving course, Bryant and his dad went with me and helped haggle a good price for a used car. Nothing too fancy. I wanted great gas mileage and safety features, and I wanted something blue. I got all three, and a whole lot more. It even came with a sunroof! I love sunroofs.

But that wasn't my biggest surprise. Our new school was small, but fun. And most of the teens there were pretty welcoming. Bryant, of course, had friends the very first day—but then again, so did I. Real, actual friends who were girls. Girls who didn't care if my hair wasn't perfect, or my shoes didn't match. Girls I could laugh with and do things with.

Bryant's oldest sister, MacKenzie, took me aside and helped me with social skills—basically how to communicate without accidentally offending people. But she also taught me that I was funny and a great listener, and someone people actually wanted to be around. It was such a new experience for me—turning into a girl again. Not that I went out and did a ton of shopping, because I honestly still couldn't stand the mall, but I could talk and laugh and enjoy myself when the girls and I were together. I miraculously grew a family within my friends too.

I belonged. I couldn't believe it.

In many ways, it reminded me of when I was younger and would play with dolls and climb trees and giggle uncontrollably for no reason.

A month before school ended, Bryant blew me away. We'd developed a deep bond, one where he was still my best friend. He still made my heart flutter every time I was near him, but we didn't kiss, or hold hands, or any of it.

However, Dr. Bailey must've liked how well I'd healed because he secretly gave Bryant the green light to surprise me. After school, we'd driven to a small ice cream shop—our favorite—and were arguing over the different points in Mr. Addington's debate class. Honestly, I can't even remember what the argument was about—knowing us, probably politics. Anyway, my sundae came, and at the bottom was a small plastic container. Like one of those things you get out of gumball machines that have a little ring or toy in them.

"What's this doing in here?" I fished it out, a bit worried, hoping I hadn't eaten anything weird.

"Do I have one?" Bryant made a pretense of looking through the rest of his sundae and then shrugged. "Nope. Open it and see what's inside. Maybe you got a prize or something."

"There's never been one before." I was about to take it up to the counter and ask about it, but curiosity got the better of me. Might as well open it first and then take it up to the counter.

It popped open easy enough, and a paper came out. "It's a note!" I unfolded it and should've realized something when I noticed Bryant's grin, but honestly, I had no idea until I read it.

Cinderella,
Will you do me the honor of going to prom with me?
I promise to behave as princely as possible.
Love,
Bryant

"Prom?" My jaw dropped, and I probably squealed. "Are you serious? You had them put this in here?"

He laughed and nodded. "All me. So, will you go?"

"Is your dad okay with it?"

"Yep. He said you're doing so well, we might as well have fun together."

"Are you serious?"

"Yes."

"Gah! I can't believe I'm going to prom! I never thought I would."

"Oh, prom definitely would've happened for you. I just can't believe I'm lucky enough to be the guy you go with."

Clarise never would have let me leave the house, but there was no reason to bring that up. I was in a different reality now. My life was so much better. And I officially got Bryant back, too. Scrambling around the table, he picked me up and hugged me for the first time in months. And I was happy. Oh, so wonderfully happy.

• • •

Until I pulled back. "Wait. Do I have to wear stupid heels? Because that so isn't happening. I'll do the dress, but please don't make me wear the shoes too."

Bryant laughed and swung me around—thankfully, we didn't hit anyone. "I love you," he said. "I love everything about you. And I don't care what shoes you wear—come in combat boots. I just want to go with you."

Chapter 22

The day of the prom was magical. I found a gorgeous yellow dress—it was vintage and retro and perfect, with layers and layers of light, fluffy tulle that swished as I walked. MacKenzie, Bryant's older sister, found a gorgeous crystal-encrusted headband and helped put my hair up. I wasn't into the whole going-to-the-salon thing, but it didn't matter because she was just as good as any actual hairdresser. I felt like a fairy princess as I floated around my room.

I'd chosen the pretty green-and-purple bedroom next to the girls months ago. There was a white bed and a white dresser and a white desk and a white mirror—they reminded me of the set from my mom. It was so fun. And girly. But not overly-pink girly, just feminine. I felt alive in that room, especially with my new dress.

I grinned as I swished back and forth in front of the mirror, watching the dress hit a few inches above my ankles. When it was time to go, I opened the box to a brand-new pair of black Converse. They weren't high-tops—I'd opted for a more flattering look and chose slip-ons.

I did a quick spin in front of my mirror, admiring my cute shoes. The whole shebang, from the sparkly tiara headband, to the fluffy vintage dress, to the Converse. I couldn't have chosen something more me and more fun if I tried.

Bryant was waiting for me as I practically skipped down the stairs. Having shoes you could walk in was a major plus. He grinned as he strode forward and met me at the bottom step. "Every time I see you, I fall a little more in love with you."

"Good." I gave him a cheeky smile. "I like to know I still have my superpowers."

He laughed and handed me a beautiful corsage of yellow roses, with sprigs of blue flowers.

"Wait!" Jeff hollered from his study. "Are you two doing all the prom stuff without me?"

When my eyebrows rose, Bryant whispered, "He wants to take pictures."

"Oh." Pictures. I'd forgotten all about those.

We endured several poses, including the official slipping-the-corsage-on-my-wrist one. Jeff was sadly charming in his own way, but really? I'd much rather get on with it!

"How about in two more minutes, we just make a run for it?" Bryant murmured in my ear.

"Two? Let's do it now!" I answered.

"Hey, I heard that." Jeff grinned and clicked one final picture. "Fine. You can go now. And have fun!"

We bolted out the door before he changed his mind. Bryant drove us to my new favorite restaurant. It was Italian, and so good. We ordered from the sweetheart menu—something they brought out for Valentine's Day and prom. After many giggles, we abandoned our half-eaten dessert and headed for the dance.

They'd rented out a large building in the center of town and decorated it with pretty twinkle lights. The whole place was like a fairy tale as we presented our tickets at the door and walked in. Our new friends rushed us and teased Bryant about his outrageous yellow tie. It was vintage and paisley, and that's all anyone needed to know about that.

But thankfully, we were left alone once a slow song came on. Bryant swirled me out in the middle of the floor and swayed to the music. He wasn't the best dancer, but he was mine, and it didn't matter to me if he stepped on my feet or was off the beat. All that mattered was that his smile was for me.

"Do you have any idea how beautiful you look tonight?" His gaze tugged at mine.

"I have no idea—what I do know is that for the first time in years, I actually feel beautiful."

"Do you?"

"Yeah. And it's all because of you."

"No." He surprised me with our first real kiss. My insides completely melted—and for the record, his kiss was way better than any of his hugs. "It's all because of you. Your bravery, your zest for life, your ability to shake off the negative. You are radiant now because you chose to be happy and forgive your past."

"A little deep for tonight, isn't it?" I chuckled and rested my cheek on his chest.

He held me tightly against him for a moment and then said, "Even your forgiveness of me—about your cat—shows how amazing you are. If it wasn't for that, we wouldn't be here now. You have chosen happiness. So many people don't, and look what they'd miss out on."

"I love my philosopher."

Bryant stepped back and looked down at me. "Did you just say what I think you said?"

Grinning, I said, "I love you, Bryant Bailey. I love how wise you are and wonderful you are—but mostly, I love how you cared about me and taught me how to love again."

"*You* taught you how to love again."

"I learned to hope, which led to living again, which allowed me to let go and fall in love." My arms wrapped around his middle. "I can see what you mean. I'm so grateful you were there and didn't give up on me. Thank you." Then I unwrapped my arms, stood on tiptoe, and pulled his head down to mine. For that bit of time, we'd forgotten anyone else was in the room.

Life was simply perfect. And it was about time.

THE END

About the Author:

Jenni James is a bestselling author with over thirty-five published books, including The Jane Austen Diaries (*Pride & Popularity, Northanger Alibi, Emmalee, Persuaded, Mansfield Ranch,* and *Sensible & Sensational*) as well as The Jenni James Faerie Tale Collection (*Cinderella, Beauty and the Beast, Sleeping Beauty, Snow White, The Frog Prince*, and many more...)

Jenni has wowed fans around the world with her unique voice in children, teen, and adult literature today, always keeping her books clean and wildly addicting. When she isn't writing, she can be found chasing her rambunctious kids around the house. She lives with her family in Utah and secretly dreams of becoming a ninja or pirate one day.

Jenni loves to hear from her fans.

Email: thejennijames@gmail.com

Snail Mail: PO Box 449, Fountain Green, UT 84632

Facebook: The Jenni James

Instagram: Author Jenni James

Twitter: Jenni_James

www.thejennijames.com

And now for a special sneak peek at *Cinderella* from the Jenni James Faerie Tale Collection, with a note from the author:

"I love Cinderella so much, I had to create a modern retelling too. If you love unique Cinderella stories as much as I do, here is the first chapter of a Cinderella I wrote back in 2013 for my Faerie Tale Collection. It is every bit a glittering fairy tale, with endless romance and love and glass slippers too! Enjoy."

Love,

Jenni James

CHAPTER ONE

ELLA PICKED UP THE last basket of clothing, her arms strained from attempting to carry the heavy, wet mass the twelve or so feet to the drying line. Thankfully, her stepmother had the gardener place the line closer to the house and in its shade, due to the sun fading her clothes, or Ella would have had to walk even farther from the washing room. Most fine houses used the drying lines inside, but Lady Dashlund preferred to have hers outside on warm days, so making the work twice as hard for Ella.

As Ella shook out the last of the petticoats, she overheard her stepsister Jillian shriek.

Oh, dear. She probably saw a mouse.

Ella sighed and quickly snapped the lacy fabric onto the line. Tossing in the remaining pins, she picked up the basket and ran toward the large manor home. No doubt they would all be in an uproar, and upset if they could not find her.

Another shriek rang out, loud and shrill, as Ella slipped off her outer shoes in the entrance near the servants' quarters and hung the wet apron to dry on one of the wooden pegs mounted upon the stone wall. She could clearly hear her stepmother shouting by the time she managed to wrap another clean apron around her waist and head up the servants' stairs.

Brushing and smoothing her dress with her hands as she went, Ella tried to remain calm. That summer, it had been especially difficult to keep the mice population down. The whole kingdom suffered from the vermin, and her stepmother and stepsisters seemed to take the sight of them the hardest. Ella was the only one of the four brave enough to try to catch them, and she had better do so quickly before her stepmother's temper got the best of her family. That was all she needed—Lady Dashlund in a foul mood. Then the whole house would pay for several days.

As she rounded the corner into the large, immaculate corridor, her feet tread upon the fine, lush carpet her father had chosen. The sumptuous rugs from the Orient lavishly displayed throughout the rooms were one of the final improvements he had made to the house before he passed on a few years back. Her heart lurched. Oh, how she missed that man. How there were days when she truly needed him near her.

Ella approached the drawing room and attempted one last time to make herself presentable before she entered. She was rather surprised to hear joyous sounds coming from within. Taking a step into the room, she beheld Jillian and Lacey laughing quite loudly and dancing about together like small girls.

Finding her stepmother across the way near the rose-colored settee, she walked up and curtsied. "Is there anything I can do for you? I heard the shouting and came as quickly as possible."

Lady Dashlund shooed her with a wispy white handkerchief, a rather large smile upon her face. "No, no. We are not in need of anything. We are all quite elated. You are welcome to continue with your chores—we will call you when we need you."

It was then that Ella noticed the small missive in her stepmother's hand. They must have had some good news. Curious, but not willing to risk Lady Dashlund's wrath, she simply said, "Yes, milady." Ella nodded, dipped into a short curtsy, and turned to go.

"No." Miss Lacey Dashlund halted in mid-twirl and put her foot down to catch her balance. "Ella cannot go just yet. We *do* need her, Mother. *Think*—the duke is coming here in only a few minutes. We need everything to look splendid! He is coming! He is coming! And this time—this time I shall finally secure him." Lacey squealed and shrieked loudly, and then picked up her sister's arm and began dancing about again.

"Girls, enough," scolded Lady Dashlund, though she was smiling. "It is time you freshen up and stop gallivanting around or you will be quite flushed when he comes."

Miss Dashlund twirled Jillian out in a final spin and then giggled with her as they stopped their play. "Oh, is it not the most glorious day?" She smiled and waltzed her way to the settee, clasping her mother's hands within her own.

"Yes. It is." Lady Dashlund grinned at her daughter before turning toward Ella. "Will you please let Cook know to send up tea as soon as the duke arrives, and make sure she adds a little something special—something to make him stay this time."

"Yes."

"Oh, and when you are through, please sweep off the front step. We do not want him walking up to the house when it looks such a sight."

"Yes, milady." Ella curtsied again and rushed from the room. She would have to be quick to clean off the whole of the front steps before the duke arrived. Lord Gavenston rarely came late. In fact, more often than not, he was early.

She hoped for his sake and Lacey's that her stepsister would not blunder this meeting like she had previously. Ella winced. Lacey was always incredibly graceful—unless His Grace was around. And then, quite simply, she became a bumbling buffoon and would somehow or another cause great catastrophes. Hopefully, this time all would be well. Ella crossed her fingers for luck just in case. After all, the sooner Miss Dashlund was gone from the house, the fewer chores Ella would have to do for her silly stepsister.

***

"OH, NO! YOU ARE not getting me to step foot into that house." His Royal Highness Prince Anthony chuckled as he drew in the reins on his beautiful horse, causing him to stop in his tracks about a half mile down the road that would eventually lead them to Lady Dashlund's rather exquisite manor. The manor, he could tolerate. It was the family that made him shudder.

"But you promised," Lord Gavenston replied, drawing in his rather fine black as well.

Anthony shook his head. "No, I did not. I promised to accompany you on some errands, Cousin. I did not promise to waltz myself into *that* home and be prodded and fawned over like some ninny. Why, those girls could cool the east, lowering the temperature a whole two degrees with their eyelash fluttering alone." The prince ridiculously fluttered his own lashes. They were on the most glorious of roadways, with fine green hills and rows of delicious apple and sturdy oak trees, some of the greatest lanes in all the kingdom, and here he was—looking the fool instead of enjoying the marvelous countryside.

Zedekiah laughed. "You are quite awful, you know."

"I kno-ow!" he replied in a singsong voice, the type reserved for pantomimes.

"And you look like a nincompoop." Zedekiah clicked his tongue and tapped his mount to press onward. "I, for one, would not wish to be seen with you if you are to act this way."

"I cannot. I simply cannot do it," Anthony replied as he tapped his horse as well. "My mother would have my head if she knew I had even spoken to them, let alone stepped in their house—and you know it!"

"This is why I had to sneak you away, so you would accompany me." Zedekiah looked over as Anthony came up. "The queen forces me to run these errands because she and Lady Dashlund were schoolgirls together. She does it to pay particular courtesy to her longtime friend. But she would rather be dead than seen conversing with the woman, which is why I, as the duke, must be her go-between. And honestly, I wish anything—anything—other than this task."

"I pity you, but I cannot risk it. They would devour me in a heartbeat."

"Come! You have not been here for ages—a good five years at least. They may have grown since then."

The prince crowed. "Yes, and this is why you need me to hold your hand. Because they are such proper ladies and behave so well! No, my mother has told me anecdotes about what the family has done to the royal castle alone. I have sheets and sheets written to me of nonsense this Miss Dashlund has done—do you have any idea how much it cost my mother to host them the last time they came? The number of shrubs she had to replace because of that girl's foolishness?"

"Which is why I need someone with me now. I would rather come out of there in one piece!" Zedekiah begged. "Please?"

Anthony stared at him as their horses rounded the corner of the lane. The great house was about forty feet in front of them. He looked up and then reached over, his hand waving his cousin to a halt. "Who is that on the steps?" he asked quietly as both horses stopped.

"I do not know." Zedekiah peered at the girl Anthony indicated. "She looks like a maid of some sort. Why?"

"Because I could swear it is Ella."

For more information Check out Jenni's books at:

Facebook: The Jenni James

Instagram: Author Jenni James

Twitter: Jenni_James

www.thejennijames.com